The Enemy Has a Face

Gloria D. Miklowitz

Eerdmans Books for Young Readers
Grand Rapids, Michigan • Cambridge, U.K.

Text © 2003 by Gloria D. Miklowitz
Published in 2003 by Eerdmans Books for Young Readers
An imprint of Wm. B. Eerdmans Publishing Company
255 Jefferson S.E., Grand Rapids, Michigan 49503
P.O. Box 163, Cambridge CB3 9PU U.K.

03 04 05 06 07 08 09 10   8 7 6 5 4 3 2 1

Library of Congress Cataloging-in-Publication Data
Miklowitz, Gloria D.
The enemy has a face / written by Gloria Miklowitz.
p. cm.
Summary: Netta and her family have relocated temporarily from Israel to Los
Angeles, and when her seventeen-year-old brother disappears, she becomes
convinced that he has been abducted by Palestinian terrorists.
ISBN 0-8028-5243-2 (hardcover : alk. paper)

[1. Missing persons—Fiction. 2. Arab-Israeli conflict—Fiction.
3. Palestinian Arabs—Fiction. 4. Jews—United States—Fiction.
5.Los Angeles (Calif.)—Fiction.] I. Title.

PZ7.M593 En 2003
[Fic]—dc21
2002009233

Book design by Matthew Van Zomeren

For my wonderful granddaughters,
Sabina and Ariana, budding authors

Author's Note

Many people became friends during the research necessary to understand the Arab-Israeli conflicts. Among them are Libby and Len Traubman, leaders in Arab-Israeli dialog who put me in touch with Israeli and Palestinian teens through e-mail contact. Among those are Netta Corren, Yona Kaplan, and Karen Kamiol-Tambour. Officer Joe Perez of the Pasadena, California, Police Department explained the procedure for filing reports on missing persons. Middle East students at Palm Middle School in Los Angeles shared with me their experiences living in the United States. Muslim middle school director Amira Al-Sarraf answered my questions about American-Muslim attitudes and lifestyles. I am grateful to all of these people and others who made this book possible.

Chapter One

Adam's voice is my alarm clock. Usually I hear the radio in the kitchen and my brother talking with Ima, that's Mom in Hebrew, before he rushes off to catch the school bus. This morning the house is deadly still. My heart almost stops when I realize what it might mean.

Before he left for school yesterday, we had breakfast together, and he was teasing Ima about a double chin—which she doesn't have! He seemed especially happy. He was wearing the silk shirt he got for his seventeenth birthday. He'd slicked down his curly brown hair and smelled so much of Moroccan Nights aftershave that I held my nose. "I may be out for dinner," he said. "I could be late."

In Israel, Adam sometimes wasn't home for dinner, no questions asked. He hung out with friends, mostly guys like him who would be in the army in another year. But girls, too. Here, in Los Angeles, we didn't have any friends yet.

1

"Where're you going?" I asked him.

"Wouldn't you like to know," he said, blushing.

．　．　．

I hurriedly dress and go into the kitchen.

"Adam didn't come home last night," Ima says. She's wearing her old bathrobe and sitting at the dinette table clutching a cup of coffee. She looks like she hardly slept. Abba, that's Dad, is on the phone. They were up most of the night phoning hospital emergency rooms she tells me, and searching Adam's room for phone numbers of possible friends. And now Abba's speaking to the police.

"No, officer!" he barks, as if the question is so idiotic it doesn't deserve a civil answer. "I know my son. He wasn't having problems at school. Or at home!"

"Sssh, Ben, please!" Ima whispers.

"He wasn't depressed! He wasn't on drugs! Believe me! And he wouldn't run away!" Abba's face reddens and he turns his back to us. His voice goes shrill. "Yes! I want to make a report! Yes, I'd like you to come here right away! Well, thank you!" He hangs up.

For a long moment he doesn't speak. I notice how his hair is growing thin and the furrows in his brow are deeper. I sit down beside Ima and wait. Finally he says, "He's a

2

teenager, they say. Raging hormones and that kind of thing. They think he's probably out with some girl, having such a good time that he forgot about everything else."

"Maybe," I say quietly. "When he left yesterday I wondered if he had a date. He had that sheepish look he sometimes gets when he's got a secret. And Mom? Remember how he was dressed up?"

Ima nods.

"Maybe the police are right. Maybe he cut school and met some girl. And they went some place. And . . . and . . . they made out. And . . . he fell asleep." I feel uncomfortable saying what makes Adam seem so— sexual. My parents listen and watch intently, wanting to believe.

The phone rings.

Abba grabs it, his eyes blazing with hope. "Adam?" he shouts. "Is that you?" He frowns and slams down the receiver. "Damn salesmen!"

"What should we do?" Ima asks.

"You're going to stay here and wait by the phone. The police won't be here for an hour or more. I'm going to his school to speak with his teachers. Maybe they know something. Maybe they saw him leave with someone."

3

Dad nods to me. "And you, young lady, better get your things together or you'll be late for school."

I want to beg, *"Please! Let me stay! Adam's my brother, and I love him too!"* But it's hopeless. When Abba gets that intimidating tone of voice, there's no arguing.

I go off to school without breakfast, too worried to care about food. Adam isn't some flake. Back home, you could always count on him. If he said he was going to be someplace at a given time, he would be there. If he expected to stay overnight with a friend, he'd phone. Why hasn't he called? Is he hurt? Is he dead?

Something bad has happened to my brother. I know it and feel helpless.

Chapter 2

At school, the seventh and eighth graders buzz happily together outside, waiting for the bell to ring, oblivious to my existence. I go off by myself, glad that no one ever notices me because today I carry a load of unshed tears that threaten to spill out at the slightest kindness.

I want to ditch classes and go home to Ima. She needs me. She wouldn't be like Abba and insist I go back to school. Or maybe I should try to find Adam on my own, but where? Los Angeles is a big city. Where would I start?

When the bell rings I move into the building like a sleepwalker, irritated with myself for always being so obedient. I sit in my classes, staring out of the windows, my thoughts elsewhere. I glare at the door, willing it to open with a messenger from the office telling me there's a phone call about Adam. But no one comes.

At lunch break I carry my tray past the noisy, crowded tables to an almost empty place in back of the cafeteria and sit apart from the few students nearby. Today's special is a cheese enchilada with rice and beans. I poke around in the brown mess and wonder if Adam is eating; the thought brings a heaviness to my chest.

The Palestinian boy in my English class is looking for a place to sit. I told Adam he scares me because every time I see him he reminds me of photos back home of suicide bombers—Arab kids who pack explosives under their clothes and set them off in crowded places to kill Israelis. Themselves, too. Our eyes lock and he heads towards me, as if daring me to turn him away.

Not you, I think. *Not now. Sit somewhere else!* But most tables, of course, are packed tightly with kids who save seats for their friends. They don't want him beside them any more than they want me. We're outsiders. Because we're new? Because we're a little different? Who knows why.

Adam never speaks of being an outsider. He doesn't seem to care that kids make fun of his accent. Maybe it doesn't bother him because he is on the high school soccer team and one of their most valuable players.

Without a word the Palestinian boy, Laith al Salaam, lays his tray down almost opposite me and slides onto the bench. He pulls a book with Arabic letters on its cover from his backpack and starts reading while forking the rice and beans.

He's in America on some kind of scholarship program, living with an Muslim family. I know because we had to write about ourselves at the beginning of the term. He's from Ramallah, the Arab city on the West Bank of the Jordan River, where all the trouble is. Where the Intifada—the Arab underground—rules.

Laith is thin and not very tall with the dark hair and eyes of most Arabs. We're from the same part of the world, which should give us lots in common, but it doesn't. He's the enemy. Palestinians hate Israelis. And Israelis have no love for Palestinians.

"There are good ones and bad ones, just like good Jews and bad Jews," Abba told me.

"Sure," I said. "They want our land. They want to kill us. I should like them? I should trust them?"

This is dumb, I decide, poking at the brown stuff on my plate. There's no use staying here; I can't concentrate. I'm going home. By now the police may be there.

I climb off the bench, sling my backpack over one shoulder and pick up my tray.

"You forgot something," Laith says. I'm startled to hear

7

him speak in Hebrew and swing around. What chutzpah! Does he think I'm leaving because of him?

He nods at a notebook someone left on the table. His dark eyes bore into me, insolent and accusing.

"It's not mine," I answer.

"Inshallah. As Allah wills it." He lowers his eyes to the book he is reading and I scoot off to empty my tray and head home.

■   ■   ■

It's one o'clock when I leave the school. The neighborhood is quiet, except for the occasional trucks or cars that swish by. And it's hot for December, like it is sometimes in Israel this time of year. As I stride along the empty streets, I find myself straining to see into every car. Is Adam being driven to some house where he will be kept for ransom? Is he wandering around, not knowing who he is because he was hit on the head and lost his memory like sometimes happens in soap operas?

We've always been close, my brother and I. He taught me to ride a bike. On my last birthday he gave me an old guitar he bought at a secondhand store and secretly converted to electric. I can gripe about school and about Ima and Abba as much as I want without Adam putting me down.

Ima looks hopeful when I open the door, but it's only me, not Adam, and her face quickly pales. She doesn't berate me for cutting school. In fact, I think she's glad I'm home.

I drop my books on the couch. "Any news? Did the police come?"

"Not yet." She strides back and forth across the living room floor, ringing her hands.

"Did Dad phone?"

She nods. "He found out that Adam cut school yesterday. Nobody saw him and he wasn't at soccer practice, either. " She starts to cry. "Why? It's just not like him! Where would he go that he had to keep it a secret from us? And why isn't he back?" She drops down onto a dinette chair and holds her face.

"Aw, Mom. Don't." I go behind her chair and hug her, pressing my cheek against her hair. But I want to cry, too. It *doesn't* make sense. Why *hasn't* Adam come home?

"We never should have left Israel!" Ima rages. "I didn't want to come. I told your father to wait until Adam finished high school and went into the army. I told him middle school is a cruel time for children, that it would be especially hard on you to make the change. I told him my parents are getting old and need me." She throws up her hands. "Did he listen? No. It's always what he wants, not what I want!"

"It isn't so hard for me, Mom," I lie because I don't like to hear her say bad things about Abba. "And Adam's been doing well."

Ima turns back and glares at me. *"Doing well? Does he have any friends? I haven't seen them! Does he get phone calls?* Sure, from friends in Israel. All he does is come home and sit down in front of his computer until bedtime. Is that—*doing well?"*

"Did you check his computer?" I ask. "I know you and Abba went through things in his room, but what about the computer?"

Ima frowns. "Last night, we tried. We went over every little piece of paper on and in his desk. Nothing. Your father tried to get into his e-mail but couldn't find his password."

"Maybe I can." I hurry to Adam's room and Ima follows. Adam's room is organized and neat, like he is. Bed made. Clothes hung. Books stacked alphabetically on shelves above the papers on his desk. Posters on the wall of Israeli rock bands and photos of his friends, some in army uniform. The printer beside the computer with its yellow light always glowing. The scent of his aftershave lingering in the room.

I sit on the swivel chair in front of that computer and Ima hovers over me. Often, when I had a school project, I'd come to Adam and he'd show me how to find information on the Internet. I try to picture Adam's fingers flying over the keys but they moved so fast I could never figure out what he typed. Besides, I never *tried* to figure it out. Adam and I trusted each other.

"How can we possibly get into his e-mail without his password?" I sit back down and stare at the computer screen. "Sometimes people use a word that describes what they do, like Artist or Writer or something like that. How do you think Adam would describe himself?"

Ima smiles. "Handsome. Smart. Charming."

"I know!" I say suddenly. "When he was helping me set up my own e-mail account and I couldn't think of a good password Adam told me that when he chose a word he decided it should have something to do with being Jewish, like 'Sabbath,' or 'mazeltov.'"

"Try them!"

I type "Sabbath" for his password, but the computer rejects it. I type "mazeltov" and the computer doesn't accept this word either. "What now?"

Ima bites her lip, thinking, then says, "You know? When Adam was about seven all his little friends loved to dress up in capes and pretend to be Superman or some other modern day superhero. Not Adam. He wanted to be Samson! Your dad and I used to laugh about it because Adam was such a skinny little kid, nothing like . . ."

"Samson!" I type the word and suddenly the computer comes alive. We're in! Now I can access my brother's e-mail. Ima drags a chair from across the room to sit beside me.

I click "New Mail" and find several letters. There are two from Israeli friends. They're chatty lines about what they're doing and who they're seeing but nothing that would give us a clue to my brother's disappearance. There's a letter from someone about bargain travel, which I immediately delete. Two messages from a discussion group about Arab-Israeli relations, mostly long articles and commentaries. "Delete?" I ask Ima.

"No, you'd better not."

And two e-mails from girls. The first one reads: "My

name is Jennifer and I'm in tenth grade. I like what you said in the chat room. You're from Israel? I have a cousin living in Kfar Blum. Do you know where that is? Write back soon."

A second letter is from Elly-gant, who writes: "You seem so cool! I like your picture, too. Where do you live? I'm from San Fernando Valley. Maybe we could meet sometime?"

"If it's a girl he went to meet," I say, "maybe she's the one!" I write back: "I'm Adam's sister. Have you seen him?" I click "Send" and wait, staring at the screen, hoping Elly-gant is at her computer, but nothing comes through.

Next, I click on "Old Mail" and find two dozen messages from Adam's Israeli friends and kids he seems to have met on the Internet. Many are from girls. One girl writes more often than the others and signs herself "S." She describes herself as five-four with short black hair and bangs. She grew up in Jerusalem and is three years older than Adam. Her final correspondence, sent two months ago, tells Adam they should meet in a private chat room.

Could she be the one Adam got all dressed up for, the one he doused himself with aftershave for?

I lift a pen from the coffee cup Adam keeps to hold scissors, pencils, and pens. I find paper and list each e-mail address to look into later. Finally, I check "Sent Mail." For an instant I hesitate because if anyone read my mail I'd be furious. But this is different. We need to know. Maybe there's a clue to Adam's whereabouts in the mail he sent.

With a rush of hope I click on "Sent Mail" and groan. Yes, there are lots of letters sent, but only one to "S" agreeing that from now on they should meet in a private chat room.

Who is "S?" Using her e-mail address, I type an instant message to her: "Do you know where my brother Adam is?" There is no response.

"Oh, Ima!" I cry in despair. "What has Adam been up to that he didn't want us to know?" I turn to Ima. There are tears in her eyes.

"What do we do now?"

■   ■   ■

"Rina?" It's Dad's voice. He must have come home while we were busy at the computer.

"Ben? We're in here!" Ima answers.

"I have someone with me."

I turn off the computer and follow Ima to the living room, hoping Abba won't be angry when he sees I didn't stay at school.

There's a police officer with him, which is weird because having a policeman in our home is unnatural.

"This is Detective Perez," Abba says when we join him. "He's here to take a missing person report. Detective? My wife, Rina."

Ima nods, a worried smile on her lips.

"Would you like some tea, Officer?"

"No, thanks, Mrs. Hofman," Detective Perez says.

"And this is my daughter, Netta," Abba continues. "Why aren't you in school, Netta?"

I glance at my books, ready to gather them up and take off, but the detective stops me. "Perhaps your daughter will know things about Adam that neither of you know, Mr. Hofman," he says. "Why don't we all sit down?"

We settle around the dinette table and Detective Perez takes a pen from his pocket and a sheet from a folder. It's marked Missing Person Report.

At first he fills in basic things, like Adam's name and age, his description, any identifying marks, school and grade. Then he wants to know if Adam used drugs or might have had anything to do with a gang.

I sit like a board, eyes never leaving the officer's face, clutching my hands and shocked at such questions. And then he asks something even worse. "Did Adam ever attempt suicide?"

My parents exchange horrified glances.

"Suicide is the third leading cause of death among fifteen- to twenty-four-year-olds, especially males," Perez adds when he sees the expression on my parents' faces.

"My son is a very stable young man!" Abba answers with barely controlled irritation. "He had nothing to do with gangs or drugs, and he'd never, ever consider, much less attempt, suicide."

"Netta?" Detective Perez asks, as if I might know Adam's moods better than Ima or Abba.

I tell him about yesterday, how happy Adam seemed when he left for school.

"Then perhaps he has a girlfriend?"

"None that we know of," Ima says.

"Could it be someone you might not have approved of? We have had cases where a boy and girl run away together."

Abba snorts. "No!"

"Netta?"

"I don't think so. Adam wouldn't run away."

"What about enemies?"

"Like who? We're here barely three months," Abba says. "Hardly enough time to make enemies."

"Adam is a friendly boy," Ima says. "Back home he was loved by everyone! He has no enemies."

"I can't imagine anyone hating Adam," I say. "He's caring and funny, and he gets along with everyone."

Perez writes all this down and asks for names of friends Adam might know. I tell him the name of the soccer coach, the only person Adam ever talked about. Perez says he'll speak with the coach and the team members. Finally, he asks for a recent photo of my brother, which Abba takes from his wallet. It's a happy picture of Adam on his last birthday wearing shorts, a cutoff shirt, and a baseball cap. Perez examines it, then slides it into his file.

"What happens now?" Abba asks, as the detective closes his folder and rises.

"We move quickly on missing children," he says. "This report will go out to local and national police, and we'll print up posters with Adam's picture. We'll check his school, hospitals, and morgues. Unless there's been foul play, chances are your son will be home by tonight begging forgiveness for causing you worry."

"Foul play?" Ima puts a hand to her throat.

"We have to consider every possibility, Mrs. Hofman, but from what you've all told me I don't believe anything bad has happened."

"Good!" Abba says, but I can tell he's thinking about all the bad things that can happen, things we see every day on TV news and in the L.A. Times. Drive-by shootings, kidnappings, sex crimes, murders—things that we don't have much of in Israel.

Before he leaves, Perez promises to keep in touch and urges us to be hopeful. "In a case like this the missing person usually turns up within twenty-four hours, sorry for worrying the family."

I can see that Ima believes him but Abba doesn't.

"And in the meantime?" Abba asks at the door. "What do we do?"

"Nothing for now. Let's see what we can do first."

We're all silent, washed out, really, after the officer's visit. Ima goes to make tea. Abba drops into his lounge chair and covers his eyes. I go to my room with the words *foul play* ringing in my ears. I lie down on my bed, hands under my head, and stare up at the ceiling. What if Adam's disappearance is due to foul play? *Oh Adam,* I pray; *please be safe.*

Chapter 3

Life must go on, Abba says, which means he expects me to go to school, do my homework, practice my violin, help around the house—to live as if our whole world hasn't turned upside down. And wait. They say the police in Los Angeles are good but they get hundreds of people reported missing each day. I'm sorry about those people, but the only one I care about is Adam.

So I do go off to school. I do help Ima. But I can't bring myself to practice my violin.

．　．　．

During Spanish class I slip away to the restroom because learning new vocabulary seems so unimportant. The room is empty. There's a smell of disinfectant and perfume. I lock myself in a stall, sit on the toilet lid, and cover my mouth to stifle the sobs. I'm so scared. I don't know what to do. How could I not know more about what was going on in Adam's life? I've always thought we were close. But are we? I'm always pouring out my woes and never asking how he feels.

When I leave the stall there's a girl at the washbasin brushing her hair, eyes fixed on the mirror. I wash my face and blot it with paper toweling.

"You okay?" she asks.

I nod, not trusting my voice.

She shrugs and searches in her backpack for lipstick and eyeliner. I hurry back to Spanish class.

Lunch break is the same as yesterday. I feel miserable and go off by myself to a distant table to be alone. Laith comes along again and plunks himself down opposite me. This time he doesn't open his book to read. Instead, he places his food on the table with fork to the left and knife to the right and opens a napkin before he looks across at me. Then he says, "I'm sorry about your brother."

"What?" I'm so startled that I'm sure my face breaks out in red blotches and I almost burst into tears.

"I heard about it from friends at Central High, where your brother goes. They said the police were around yesterday, asking about him. Is he back yet?"

Since when is it your business? I almost answer, because of all people, I don't expect caring from him. But he's the first person who has spoken to me about Adam, and the sympathy cuts me right through to the heart. "No, he's not home, yet," I say, swiping at my eyes with a napkin.

"That's tough. I know how you feel."

"Oh, sure!" I know it's mean to say that, but how could he possibly know how I feel?

He curls his slice of pizza and bites into it, eyes fixed on me, and doesn't speak until he's swallowed the food. "You're so typical! You Israelis treat us like we're subhuman, like we can't have feelings like you do. You think we don't have people in Ramallah disappear all of a sudden?"

"It's not the same."

"Really? In my country, Palestine, friends of mine disappear all the time. Sometimes it's because some Israeli soldier picks them up, decides they're dangerous, and hauls them off to prison. When they get out—*if* they get out—they may be missing a hand because it was cut off for throwing a stone! My uncle . . ."

I cut him short. "Bull! We don't do things like that in Israel!" I say. "And by the way, there is no Palestine. Ramallah is part of Israel!"

"Really?" Laith smiles, but it's not a friendly smile.

"You know, Netta, we're in the good old USA now. Not Israel or Palestine where you and I are not equals. We should talk sometime. We have a lot more in common with each other than with these American kids."

I don't answer.

Laith shrugs. "As they say in America—the ball's in your court."

I stare at the food on my plate. "I have to go." I gather my things together. He's watching me closely. "Thanks for the sympathy. Maybe it would be nice to talk sometime, but right now I have other things on my mind."

"Shalom," Laith says as I leave.

■ ■ ■

On the way to my last class, climbing the stairs to the second floor, my mind is on the phone call home I just made. Ima answered breathlessly, and her voice drained away when she heard it wasn't Adam. "I'll be home soon," I said, trying to lift her spirits.

I hurry down the stairs to my next class when someone nearby suddenly calls out, "Joel, wait up!" The name makes me stop with a sudden rush of excitement while kids push around me to get by. Joel. That was a name Adam mentioned from time to time. I'd forgotten! A friend in his school? Joel—Joel—what? Weiss! Maybe Adam told him something. I have to talk with him!

Ima looks terrible when I reach home. She's still in her bathrobe. Her fair skin is blotchy, and her pretty shoulder-length hair needs brushing. But when I tell her I remember a name of one of Adam's possible friends she brightens and hurries to the kitchen to find the phone book. There must be at least twenty people with the last name Weiss. I get out a map and mark which addresses might be within the school district, then start calling.

"Is Joel Weiss there?" I ask whenever someone answers. One after another, the answer is no. Finally, after a dozen calls, a woman answers who yells, "Joel? Phone!" A moment later I hear the woman whisper, "Some girl . . ." and then a male voice says "Hello?"

"This is Netta Hofman," I say. "Do you go to Central High?"

There's a long pause and then the boy says, "Netta Hofman? Adam's sister?"

"Yes!" I shiver with nervousness.

"I heard he's missing. Disappeared. He's not back yet? Is that why you're calling?"

I get a lump in my throat and turn away from the phone.

"It's him," I whisper to Ima.

"Ask him when he saw Adam last."

"He wasn't at school yesterday, if that's what you want to know. At least I didn't see him."

"Did he talk about going anywhere?"

"No."

"Did he seem depressed?"

"No."

"Did he talk about any special girl he liked?"

"He did tell me he met some girl on the Internet. He really seemed to like her. Said she was older but that didn't matter. Said they could talk about anything, even politics."

I grip the phone tighter in my damp hand and take a deep breath. "Do you know her name? That sounds like the girl who signed herself 'S.'"

"He never mentioned it."

"What about girls at school?"

"Girls at school? I never saw him with any particular girl, but yeah, they like him. Why not? He's funny, a good athlete, maybe a little exotic because he's from another country. And not bad looking."

I'm silent for a while, trying to think what else to ask.

And then I think of the detective's question, about enemies, and ask Joel about that.

"If you mean, like, *gangs* out to get him, no. He didn't hang with kids in gangs. But kids who didn't like him? Some. Not enemies, but guys who didn't like how he'd go on about the Middle East and wouldn't shut up. He could be pretty loud, especially if you didn't agree with him." He pauses. "Listen, Netta. I don't know why your brother's not home, but he wouldn't run away, and no one could hate him enough to hurt him."

My voice quavers. "What do you think happened to him then?"

"I don't know, but I bet he'll be home soon."

"I hope so." When there's no more to say I thank Joel who says to call him anytime if he can help. And then I hang up and stare at Ima.

Neither of us says anything but I know what she's thinking, the same as I am—that it's into the second day that Adam's been missing and this phone call was another dead end. The house seems so silent, so scarily empty. We should be doing *something* to find Adam, but what?

"Why don't you practice now, dear," Ima says.

"I can't, Mom. I just can't!" I begin to cry. It's two days

since I touched my violin and my lesson is tomorrow. Before Adam disappeared, one of the special things we did on a Friday evening was for Abba to get out his cello and Ima to sit at the piano and for me to bring in my violin. My teacher gave us special music that we could play together. We sounded pretty good. Adam called us The Hofman Trio and would always applaud when we finished.

Practice? How can I care about music right now? I don't think The Hofman Trio will want to play again until my brother comes home.

Chapter 4

Help! Help me, please! Netta! Abba! Someone— help! They're going to kill me! Oh, please, get me out of here!

I thrash about in bed. In the dream I see Adam in a dark place, a room, a cellar? His eyes are wide with fear and his shackled hands reach out. There is blood on his face and shirt and he's crying. I mumble incoherent words that in my head mean, "Where are you? Tell me!" I reach out to my brother, stretch with every muscle in my body towards him, and fall to the floor, sobbing.

Ima, in a nightgown, is quickly at my side. She gathers me in her arms. "What is it, motik, sweetie? Are you hurt? Was it a bad dream?"

I shake my head and cover my mouth, the dream still vivid. "I saw him; I saw Adam! He's in terrible trouble," I cry. "He needs our help! He's in a cellar someplace and he's tied up! He's bleeding!"

"Sssh, sssh . . ." Ima rocks me and talks softly in

Hebrew, even hums a melody she used to sing when I was a child. "It was only a dream."

"No! He was alive!" I insist. "It was real! He was trying to tell me where he is!"

"Yes, yes. I know. Dreams are sometimes like that. Go back to bed now, darling. Think good thoughts and get some sleep."

I wipe my eyes and climb back in bed. Ima tucks the blanket around me and bends down to kiss me.

"Stay, Ima," I beg. "Just a little while . . ."

Ima sits on the side of my bed and takes my hand. She pushes her auburn hair, the same color as mine, from her eyes.

"I'm awfully scared for Adam," I whisper. "How will we ever find him if he's a prisoner somewhere, like in my dream? And wouldn't whoever took him want money for his return?"

Ima smooths my forehead. "No one's contacted us for ransom."

"Could it be terrorists? Palestinian terrorists?"

"This is *America*, Netta, not Israel. No, dear. I can't believe that."

"Then why is he not home?" Just saying the words

brings fresh tears and I reach for a tissue to blot them.

We whisper together for a long time, examining every word Adam spoke in the few days before he disappeared, looking for answers. Finally, Ima rubs her eyes, kisses me again, and returns to her room. I curl up on my side and try to sleep.

■ ■ ■

It is Friday, another school day. Laith is in the cafeteria before I arrive. I see him ahead of me in line to get food, wearing a red and green T-shirt, the colors of the Palestinian flag, and it irritates me. He looks about, then finds a table apart from other students. As I leave the line I stand for a moment with my tray of food, uncertain. There are spaces to sit with others, and if I join someone I don't know maybe I could make a friend. But Laith is watching. And I think of what he said yesterday, that we should talk, that we have more in common with each other than with American kids. I go to his table where he sits apart from three other students.

"Shalom," he says, opening a container of milk, the only cafeteria food he bought. He has food from home today, stuffed grape leaves, hummus, and pita bread. On my tray is a grilled tuna sandwich, packaged potato chips, and a fruit cup.

"Any news about your brother yet?"

"No."

He frowns and his dark eyes seem more friendly. "I'm real sorry." He holds out a foil sheet with stuffed grape leaves on it and says, "They're good, even if they're store-bought. Try."

My mouth waters, but I don't want to take Laith's lunch. "I love them, but . . . no thanks." I motion at my food tray and make a face. "I do miss the food we get at home. Everything tasted better. Even Big Macs were bigger and juicier. Here, everything seems so—plastic."

The look on Laith's face as he withdraws the grape leaves makes me think that rejecting his food insults him, that maybe I think it's not clean. I reach across the table. "On second thought, I'll try one. Only one."

I take the lamb and rice-stuffed leaf in my fingers and eat it slowly, eyes closed, licking my fingers when I finish. "Yum . . . ," I announce and smile. For the first time all day I am thinking of something besides Adam.

"You know what I miss?" Laith asks. "My mother used to cook Beama. It's a stew with lamb, okra, tomatoes, rice, and pine nuts. Oh, my, so good!"

"Can't you get that here?"

"I'm living with an American-Islamic family, but the wife cooks mostly American food."

"When you go home for the summer you can enjoy all that again," I say, taking a bite of my sandwich.

He gives me a funny look.

"What?"

"I *can't* go home. *You ought to know that.* Not until you Jews let us move around freely in our country. If I could get home, I'd probably never be able to come back."

"It's all our fault? If you'd quit the violence, stop sending suicide bombers in to kill innocent people—"

He cuts me off. "Your soldiers have put up road blocks so our people can't go out or come in to our own towns— even to work. My little cousin was sick and my aunt carried him miles to the checkpoint. She begged the Israeli soldiers to let her out to take him to a hospital. They wouldn't."

"What happened?"

"My cousin died." He cocks his head and glares at me. "The soldiers said they had 'orders.'"

"I'm really sorry."

"*We're* violent? Wouldn't losing a child that way turn

you violent?"

I can see Laith's point, but what about the innocent-looking Arabs who *do* get passed through the checkpoint and end up killing innocent Jews? There's so much I could say, but it's hopeless, arguing with someone who only sees one side, the Arab side. Rather than answer his tirade I concentrate on finishing my lunch, pack up, and hurry away. I don't think I'll sit with him again.

■ ■ ■

It's Friday. The Sabbath begins at sundown. Odd that I haven't thought that in a long time. In Israel, it never seemed important to be observant because being Jewish was all around us. We didn't need to go to religious services to know who we were. But here, it's not the same. I don't feel connected. I miss the warmth of being part of my people.

Again, when I reach home, there is no news and Ima looks like she has cried all day. She has not left the house for fear of missing a phone call.

"Do you need anything from the store?"

"Some milk, maybe . . ." She bursts into uncontrollable tears and mutters how Adam could go through a gallon of milk a day.

I feel queasy and finally ask, "Where's Dad?"

"At work. He says he has to do something to get his mind off Adam for a while or he'll go crazy."

"It's Friday, Mom. Could we maybe go to temple?"

"Temple? We haven't been to synagogue since your Bat Mitzvah!"

"But maybe . . . it would help."

"How?"

"I don't know."

"You know we can't leave the house! What if Adam phones? What if the police want us?" Her voice breaks.

"Ima, don't." I go into the kitchen. "I'm going to fix us some tea. I bet you haven't eaten since breakfast."

"I don't want anything." She comes into the kitchen and hugs me while I fill the teapot with water. "I'm sorry, honey. Maybe Abba will go to temple with you. You could pray. Maybe it would help."

■　■　■

"Nothing new," Abba says when he comes home. He always embraces Ima, but tonight his hug is quick and preoccupied. "Perez says he'll have flyers tomorrow and will bring some by for us to post in the neighborhood. I'm thinking that maybe we should hire a private detective."

"Wash up, Ben, and come eat. We'll talk about it at dinner. You, too, Netta." Ima is trying to make things normal. She has put on a fresh dress but no makeup to hide the dark shadows under her eyes. The table is set for four even though Adam isn't here. I don't ask why, but she explains anyway. "Who knows? Maybe the bell will ring and there he'll be." She begins to cry, and Abba murmurs, "Sssh, sssh . . . it will be all right."

None of us has the appetite for the meal she prepared—a typical Friday night dinner of roast chicken, kasha, string beans, and a fruit compote with cookies for dessert.

I sit in my usual place, but the chair opposite me, Adam's seat, is empty. Abba glances at it from time to time, and the wrinkles in his forehead deepen. Dinner was always lively with conversation and food passed around when Adam was home. Abba would talk about people he met at work. Ima would ask us about school. We laughed. We argued. We talked about everything, sometimes all at once.

But tonight, even though we try to be normal, there are awkward silences. Conversation flows and ebbs half-heartedly, going nowhere, as our minds return to the only thing that matters: Adam. Without my brother, we are not complete.

"Netta would like to go to temple tonight," Ima says.

"Sure, go. I'll stay by the phone."

There's a lot of back and forth stuff about who should stay, but Abba wins. "Rina, dear, you need to get out of the house for a while," he says. "It will do you good."

■ ■ ■

It's weird, the two of us walking into the synagogue without Abba. We don't know anyone, and we've never been here before. Friends cluster, greeting each other, just like at school, but some nod at us and say "Shalom" and "Good Shabbos" as we pass. I recognize a girl from my English class and think maybe I'll talk with her on Monday.

The sanctuary is a pleasant room with wooden benches and stained glass windows showing Bible scenes. Large flower displays brighten the bima, the stage. We read from prayer books in Hebrew and English, and a small choir sings sorrowful, beautiful melodies. I am glad we came. I feel connected and at peace for a time.

"Let's go," Ima murmurs, right after the rabbi's sermon. She does not want to stay for refreshments and forcefully presses me towards the exit, avoiding eye contact with others to prevent conversation. I guess she's not ready to speak of our loss and take solace from strangers. Maybe she's ashamed to say her son has disappeared, maybe run away. Or maybe she just wants to get home in hopes there's news of Adam.

"Ima, wait!" I whisper. "Maybe we should speak with the rabbi. He may have contacts with other congregations who can put out the word to look for Adam!"

"Not now, Netta!" Ima replies, hurrying along. When I try to persuade her she says, "Don't argue! Come!"

When we get to the car Ima gropes for the keys. "I have this feeling," she explains, "that Adam is back! We have to get home!"

She drives fast, a smile on her lips all the way, while I clench the shoulder strap like it's a lifeline. Can it be? Is it possible? Is our nightmare over?

■ ■ ■

There is no greater letdown than expectation that doesn't come to pass, like a party you look forward to for weeks, and it's canceled. Like coming home, expecting Adam to be back—and finding he's still missing.

CHAPTER 5

Detective Perez is at our door Saturday morning with a stack of flyers. There is a picture of Adam on each, and the words, "Have you seen this boy? Age, 17. Height, 5'10". Weight, 155 pounds." A toll-free number for the police is listed on the bottom.

Ima brings coffee to the table and we all sit down. I feel uncomfortable when Perez takes Adam's usual seat.

We lean towards the detective as if he's whispering, yet his voice is perfectly clear. It's just that he's talking a lot but not saying much to give us hope. I remember Adam once observing that people who blabber on about nothing are either empty-brained or trying to hide something.

Abba taps his finger on the table. "You're saying you have no new leads? Is that right?" he asks, then glances anxiously at Ima, "Not even any . . . bodies you haven't identified?"

Ima draws a deep breath and closes her eyes. I get a rush of sudden cold.

"Mr. Hofman, please. It's early yet," Perez says.

"Early? I thought the chances of finding someone who's disappeared get poorer with each day!" Abba glares at Perez and then adds, "We're going to hire a private detective. What do you think of that?"

"I understand. I have a daughter your son's age. If she disappeared, I'd do the same. We'll do everything we can to cooperate with whoever you hire."

"Is there anything else we can do?" I ask, softly.

"You can post these flyers . . ."

"Of course!" Abba answers, as if Perez insults us by saying the obvious. I know he's scared, which is why he's irritable, but Perez is trying to help us so Abba shouldn't be so nasty.

"You can check his computer and contact everyone he has written to or received messages from."

"We started to do that," I say in a tiny voice and realize I didn't follow up on Elly-gant or any of the other e-mails that might lead somewhere. "I'll do that today."

"Good. Any other questions? If not, I'll be on my way." Detective Perez sets his coffee down and slides the stack of flyers towards Abba.

"Just . . ." I stare at my clenched hands because I'm

afraid the detective will laugh at me. "I had a dream. I know it sounds crazy," I hurry to add, "but I saw Adam in a cellar someplace. He was hurt and he couldn't get out."

Perez doesn't laugh. "I'm no psychologist, but I'd guess the dream is your subconscious searching for answers to your brother's disappearance," he says.

My eyes blur when I look up. "But, what if it's true? My brother and I were very close! Sometimes I think he could read my mind!"

"If he's a prisoner someplace, if he was abducted, we should have heard from his captors by now with whatever they want in return for Adam, Netta."

"But it's possible, isn't it?"

"Anything's possible."

"Could we—maybe—go on television, or something? Tell how we feel? Ask people to call if they saw him with anyone?"

"Yes!" Ima exclaims.

"That's possible," Perez says.

"Will you see how we go about doing that?" Abba asks as the detective stands to leave.

■   ■   ■

It's Saturday, and we spend the rest of the morning

tacking the flyers on telephone poles and asking local shop owners for permission to tape them in their windows.

Later, we drive to Central High and do the same in that area. It's a strange feeling, walking the streets that Adam walked, like Adam is near. I wonder if Ima and Abba feel as I do.

We stop at a coffee shop two blocks from the school for permission to leave a flyer. I get an even stronger feeling that Adam has been here, though the manager doesn't remember anyone who looked like the person in the photo.

"You can't depend on 'feelings,'" Abba says. "Adam had a bus to catch after school each day so he wouldn't have had time to hang around a coffee shop."

■　■　■

Back home, Abba calls private investigators from a list Perez gave him. I go to Adam's computer to check for new mail and to contact his chat room buddies. I'm not even sure what I'm looking for. A threat? A correspondence that went sour? A love interest? What I do find is that Adam may not have made friends at school but he certainly had a lot of friends on the Internet.

One kid mostly sends him jokes—like the minister, the priest, and the rabbi who go to a funeral and each of them owe the dead man $1,000. The minister drops ten one-hundred dollar bills in the casket. The priest does the same. The rabbi, however, writes a check for $1,000 and drops that in the casket.

Ha ha.

Girls write about TV programs where all the female characters are gorgeous and sexy and wind up in bed with the boys. Are they suggesting that's what they want from Adam?

Some of the guys talk about sports, others about classes they like or hate, movies they see, girls they like.

Did Adam write back to any of them?

I'm beginning to feel the computer network leads nowhere, but before turning it off, I accidentally jar the keyboard so it moves a little. A flash of yellow catches my eye. It's a small Post-it note under the keyboard. I slide it out and find the name Sari written on it. Not only once, but several times, with a heart around the largest one.

"Ima!" I call out. "Come! I found something!"

Ima hurries to my side and takes the Post-it from my hand.

"Did he ever mention anyone by that name?" she asks. When I shake my head she asks, "Did you find any e-mails from a—Sari—or Sara?"

"No, but there was one signed 'S.' Maybe that stands for Sari. Could he have run away with her? I mean, it's just not like him, but . . ."

"Ben?" she calls. "Come see what Netta found!"

My father joins us, and he, too, studies the tiny slip. He turns it over and studies it some more, as if it has some secret message in the few letters. "I don't know," he says. "It's probably nothing, but on the other hand . . . I'll call Perez and see what he thinks."

■ ■ ■

On Sunday, my parents interview a private detective while I hang around, thinking I should do the book report that's due or practice my violin for the concert my teacher has planned for his students. I don't want to do either of those things. The phone rings, and I get that expectant, hopeful feeling as I run to answer it. But it's not Adam. It's Joel, who asks if there's anything new.

I tell him about the flyers we distributed yesterday, and of the note I found with the name Sari written all over it. "Did you ever hear Adam mention that name?"

"I don't think so," he says. And then, "Look. I called to ask if I could help in some way."

My throat tightens because it's so kind. No one except Perez has offered help. "How?"

"I don't know. I could put up flyers where I live? If you'd like to just talk, I could come over, or meet you some place?"

"My parents and I are sticking pretty close to each other right now, Joel. They don't trust anyone."

"They couldn't distrust *me* . . ."

"No . . . but . . ." I'm thinking that Abba probably *would* distrust Joel because he'd wonder about anyone who had contact with Adam.

"If you can't, I understand . . . ," Joel, says.

"No. It's all right. I want to talk, but not around here. Where could we meet?"

"There's a coffee shop on Ventura, just where the bus stops for Central High."

"I know the place. We had lunch there yesterday. When?"

"Now?"

I have to think a moment. My parents are interviewing a private detective in the living room. I can hear their voices. If I tell them where I'm going they'll say no. Whatever happened to Adam could happen to me, too, they'll reason. "All right," I say. "I'll come. How will I know you?"

"Red hair. Brown eyes. Five-ten. Triathalon T-shirt."

I get a tingle of fear as my big brother's friend describes himself. Should I be asking him to come here instead of going to him? Should I tell my parents I'm going? No. They won't approve. Dare I disobey? "See you in a half hour," I say. "Bye."

I go through the living room where Ima and Abba are deep in conversation with a short, heavy man. "Be back soon," I murmur.

"Netta! Wait!" Ima leaves the men and hurries to me. "Who was on the phone?"

"A boy from school. He wanted to know about an assignment," I lie. "I'm just going for a walk. Be back before dark."

Ima looks unsure, like she's considering if she dares let me go out alone. But maybe she's thinking that we all need a little space from each other. "All right," she agrees. "But don't go far. And be careful."

"I'm always careful." I'm only going to see Joel, I think, in a public place. What could happen that I need to be careful?

Chapter 6

As I wait for the public bus I sit on a bench hugging myself and wondering if I should be doing this. I've never had to lie. My parents are always pretty good about where I go and who I see. In Israel they trusted that no harm would come to me as long as I stayed out of the Arab areas. With all that freedom there was no need to rebel. But in the few days since Adam disappeared the rules have changed. Ima and Abba are so fearful, it's a wonder they let me go to school.

But I can't let their paranoia change me. If Adam trusted Joel, he must be okay.

The bus finally comes, and it's almost empty. I gaze out the window at the liquid amber trees near home, stripped bare now that it's November. Sad, like our home is now.

Along Ventura Boulevard most of the shops are closed because it's Sunday. In Israel we close on the Jewish Sabbath, Saturday.

It's only a few minutes' bus ride to the coffee shop near

the high school, and as we get nearer I get more and more uneasy. When I leave the bus my legs are wobbly from fear. Who is this Joel, after all? What if he is involved in Adam's disappearance? Abba says I trust everyone, that some day I'll get into serious trouble because of it.

I arrive at the coffee shop and follow a family pushing two small children in a twin stroller through the door. Joel is seated on a bench. I know it's him because of the red hair. He seems anxious and stands up as soon as he sees me. "Netta?" he asks.

"Hi, Joel," I answer. He's an average-looking guy with freckles on very fair skin. He's wearing jeans and a green shirt with the triathalon logo on the front.

"I'm glad you came." He points to a booth along the window, and I follow him to sit down.

Now, it's awkward when we're opposite each other. I clasp my hands in my lap and try to think where to begin, what to ask. What did Joel and my brother talk about? Soccer? Classes? Girls? Life in Israel? What?

The waitress comes to our booth with a pad and pencil. Her name is Bonnie. She's a pretty blonde with a big bosom, the kind who works to pay the rent while trying to get into the movies. "What would you like?" Joel asks.

"Just hot chocolate, please."

"I'll have the same." He stares at me and says, "You don't look at all like Adam."

I self-consciously brush my hair back and shrug. "I look more like my mother."

"How long is it since Adam's been missing?"

"Five days!" My voice breaks and to cover up my upset I reach into my backpack and pull out a bunch of flyers. "I brought these. Maybe you can tack them up in school . . ."

Bonnie returns with our drinks and sets them down. She glances at the flyer.

I hold one out to her. "Keep it. He's my brother. Have you seen him? I was here yesterday, and your manager let us put one in the window."

She examines Adam's picture, then says, "A lot of high school kids come in here. I really don't pay them much attention unless they get loud or make trouble. Or, they are regulars. You know how it is. I take their orders and give them their checks. That's about it."

"Miss! Miss!" a man in a nearby booth calls.

"In a minute!" she calls back, then offers to show the flyer to the other waitresses before turning away.

Joel and I silently sip our chocolate drinks when he

asks, "Could Adam have had a mental breakdown? I mean . . . maybe he forgot who he is. Maybe he got one of these schizophrenic episodes I've read about where the person thinks he's Santa Claus or Jesus Christ or something."

"That wouldn't come on suddenly, would it? And anyway, if he was acting crazy, wouldn't he wind up in a hospital?"

"Not necessarily. He could be wandering around, eating out of garbage cans, not knowing where he lives or where he should be."

I think about Adam as a homeless person and shake my head. "We would have noticed something. The morning he left he was perfectly normal."

"Then maybe he did run off with this girl whose name you found on the note. What was her name? Sari? What kind of name is that, anyway?"

I play with the paper napkin, tearing little pieces from it so I won't have to look at Joel. "Could be Jewish. Could be American. Could be anything."

"Could it be Palestinian?"

I look up. "Why? What are you thinking?"

"If you were in Israel and this happened, you'd be thinking some terrorist Islamic group might have taken

Adam to retaliate for something Israel did."

My hands grow cold and sweaty. "But this is America!"

"I know . . . but . . ."

I tell Joel about Laith and the things we argue about, and Joel says, "Adam argued all the time with some of the kids from the Middle East in school. I told him the best thing to do was cool it. 'You're in America, now, not Israel,' I told him."

"And Adam said?"

"He complained that American kids only talk about sports and television and there's a lot more than that going on in the world that they ought to know about."

"Yeah . . . ," I say. "He used to complain about that at home."

Bonnie returns to our table with another waitress at her side who has color-streaked hair and three earrings in one ear. "This is Isabel. She thinks she saw your brother."

"When?!" I ask, feeling a rush of excitement and hope.

Isabel holds the flyer, studying it. "Last week, I think."

"When? Was he with anyone?"

"Tuesday, or Wednesday, around nine o'clock. He looked like a high school kid, and I wondered if he was cutting school because by nine in the morning the high school kids leave for classes." She smiles. "I liked his shirt." She glances behind her as if the manager might be watching.

"Did he have an accent, an Israeli accent?" Joel asks.

"I think so. He was sitting in that booth." She points to a booth near the back of the coffee shop. "There was a girl with him."

"A girl?!" Joel and I exchange excited glances.

She nods.

"Did he call her by name? What did she look like?"

"Couldn't say. She was reading the menu while he gave me their order so I didn't see her face. I kind of concentrated on him. I remember thinking he seemed very happy. He kept glancing toward the girl and smiling."

Oh, Adam, I think, with relief. You nut case. Did you have to run away without telling us you were in love? I take a deep breath and smile. "Did they stay long? Did you see if they left in a car?"

Isabel shrugs. "I didn't see them leave, just left their order and their bill and got busy with other customers." She glances behind her. "I gotta go. Anything else you want to know?"

"No, Isabel. Thanks, " I say. "You've been a really big help."

■ ■ ■

Joel and I leave the coffee shop soon afterwards, and I am elated. I can hardly wait to get home and tell Ima and Abba the news. I tell Joel that my father will be furious that Adam ran off with some girl without telling us his plans. "I can just hear him rant: 'He's only seventeen! He has to finish school! He has to return to Israel for his army duty! He can't support a wife now!'"

Joel chuckles. "Just like my dad would say."

"And I can hear Ima." I take on her voice. "'Ben, calm down! If Adam did go off with some girl he would have phoned by now. He just wouldn't leave us worrying, not after all this time. It has to be something else.'"

"What else could it be?" Joel asks as I realize what Ima would say is true.

"I don't know, Joel. It's the same thing I can't figure out."

Chapter 7

We are sitting in the living room late Sunday night with Detective Perez. The fresh flowers Ima always keeps on the piano are wilting. I want to pluck them from their vase and throw them away because they remind me of death.

"I've set up a television interview with Chuck Harris of Channel 7 News for tomorrow night," Perez informs us. "Harris doesn't usually devote time to kids who disappear, but your case is unusual. You're Israelis, for one, only here a short time. The viewing audience will want to know how come an Israeli kid with no history of problems vanishes."

Abba nods, listening intently.

"And, Dr. Hofman, your work here on satellite systems is important to the United States. Could that have anything to do with your son's disappearance?

All color drains from Abba's face. "I've considered that," he says.

Ima takes Abba's hand and kisses it. "If Ben's work was the reason, someone would surely have contacted us by now."

"Perhaps." He glances at a paper in his hand. "Well, then—this is what to expect tomorrow."

■ ■ ■

I don't go to school Monday. Instead, Perez picks us up and we drive to the television studio to be filmed for the evening news. We hardly speak, each into our own thoughts. Adam has been missing for almost a week now. I'm beginning to think we will never see him again. I go around all the time with a huge bubble of tears in my chest and pray that the bubble won't burst when I'm in front of the camera. If Adam doesn't return, how will we be able to bear it?

■ ■ ■

The makeup lady is a plump woman with silver-gray hair framing her face. She chatters about my skin and hair as she applies foundation and blush and I wish she'd shut up. The cosmetic smells almost make me puke. I keep worrying what Harris will ask me and rehearse in my mind what I will say in the few seconds I'll have before the camera.

We wait in "The Green Room" until we are taken to the studio where we meet Chuck Harris, the man who will interview us. He's seated at a table with several chairs beside him and looks older than when I've seen him on TV. Facing him is a small army of cameramen, lighting people, and others. Behind him is a huge mural of downtown Los Angeles.

I swallow a lump of fear and follow Ima and Abba to seats at the table. We're introduced to Harris and someone hooks tiny microphones to our shirts. Then Chuck Harris explains the procedure, asks if we have any questions, and suddenly we're "on."

"Good evening," Harris says, gazing seriously at the cameras. "Six days ago a seventeen-year-old Israeli boy named Adam Hofman disappeared. He left home for Central High School at the usual time but did not attend classes and has not been heard from since." The cameras cut to a photo of my brother. While the photo is on the screen Harris says, "He was last seen at a coffee shop near his school in the company of a young woman whose name may be Sari. That is all that is known about him at this time. His family believes he would not have run away. That—he might be hurt and unable to phone, or that he is the victim of foul play."

I stare ahead, hearing the words and shivering as Harris

asks the public for help. "If you have seen Adam, or have any information about his whereabouts, please telephone the number at the bottom of your screen."

Next, the camera focuses on us. Abba is used to speaking at conferences and appearing on Israeli television, so he is not nervous. Still, his face is flushed as he announces a reward of $50,000 for Adam's return.

Ima speaks next. "Please—Adam—if you are listening, call us. At least let us know you are alive!" Her voice breaks. "If you are a hostage—then I beg those who are holding you—don't hurt my son. He's a good boy. We want him back! We will do anything to get him back safely!" Her voice breaks and I reach out for her icy hand.

Now the cameras are on me. "I love you, Adam," I say, forgetting everything I planned. And then the bubble of tears bursts and I throw my hands over my face, sobbing.

■　■　■

At school the next day lots of kids who never noticed me before suddenly talk to me.

"I saw you on TV last night! Gee! I'm so sorry. I hope you find your brother."

"Thanks."

"My brother knows yours. They're both on the Central

High soccer team. He said Adam was a real good player. Is, I mean. You going to the library? I'll walk with you."

"Thanks."

"I heard your brother might be with a girl named Sari? My cousin's name is Sari, but she lives in Virginia."

Suddenly, I'm a celebrity, just because I appeared on TV and Adam is missing. Kids who never showed the slightest interest in me stop to offer condolences or ask about Adam. Is their concern genuine or just morbid curiosity? Instead of giving me comfort, each questioner opens the wound in my heart a little wider. I don't know how to answer them.

■ ■ ■

The girl I saw at the temple Friday night is in my English class. As soon as I settle at my desk she comes to me.

"I *thought* I saw you Friday night," she says. "Why didn't you stay?"

"We had to get home, in case my brother phoned." She's a pretty girl with green eyes and red hair.

"I didn't know that a terrible thing happened until I heard about you on TV and saw the posters about Adam. I'm real sorry. If there's anything I can do . . ."

"Thanks," I murmur, sliding my text from my backpack and pulling out my notebook.

"I'm Shoshana O'Hara." She extends a hand.

"O'Hara?"

She grins. "I know. It's kind of complicated. My father is Irish-Catholic, which accounts for my Irish name, but my mother is Jewish. And if your mother is Jewish . . ."

I finish her sentence, " . . . then you're legally Jewish."

She laughs. "Right. Mom and I go to synagogue Friday nights, ever since my Bat Mitzvah. Were you Bat Mitzvahed?"

"In Israel, at Masada."

"Cool!"

"Actually, it was August, so it it was very *hot*. And very, very cool!"

Her smile fades. "I don't mean to scare you, Netta, but I've been thinking about what happened to your brother and I had an idea. My Dad comes from Northern Ireland and things like that go on all the time there."

"What things?"

"You know, the violence between Protestants and Catholics? The hatred that goes way back? One side captures a member of the other and . . ."

She must see the expression of alarm on my face as I follow her reasoning—that Adam's absence might be due to Palestinian revenge. But revenge for what? We're just ordinary Israelis. We, personally, haven't done anything. And if a terrorist group is involved, they'd be sure to take credit for it, like they do in Israel.

"Maybe it's not quite the same," she hurries to correct, "but I just thought your family should explore—"

"We have! Those hate groups have power in Israel, but not here, Shoshana!" My face begins to burn. "It isn't the same. My brother's no terrorist, like you have in Ireland. No. I don't believe that."

She steps back. "I didn't say . . . I just thought . . ."

I shake my head, wanting to clear it of the new worry planted there. "I know you're trying to help, but that's way off!" I think I hurt her feelings so I add, "Thanks, though. I'll tell my parents what you said."

■ ■ ■

I mull over Shoshana's words as I move on to social studies class. Are we missing something? Adam had contact with Arab-Israeli discussion groups on the Internet. Joel said he tended to be outspoken about the Middle East and some kids didn't like him for it. But—he was last seen with a girl, not masked men with guns!

Laith is leaning against the doorjamb of my social studies class whistling softly as he watches the passing students. He straightens up as I approach and asks, "Got a minute?"

"Why?" I wish he'd leave me alone. Right now I have no interest in him or anyone from Palestine.

He moves aside. "I saw you on TV last night. Both at seven o'clock and again at ten."

Two classmates push by, glancing at us. "So?"

"It's very sad, what happened."

"So?" His kindness takes me by surprise and I blubber, "It was awful. I feel so stupid, the way I broke up, crying like that."

"You just showed how you felt. In your place, I might have done the same."

I take a deep breath. "Really?"

The teacher arrives; the bell rings, and the halls are emptying. "I better go in."

"Right." He starts away, then turns back. "Netta, wait! I'll walk you home, if you like. Meet me near the entrance after last class?"

Before I can think if I want him to, I nod. And then I go

into my social studies class.

. . .

I see Laith before he sees me and think there's something sad about him, the way he always seems to be apart from others, like now. He's slouching against a tree just outside the school entrance, watching the kids go by.

It's typical after-school chaos. Two boys throwing frisbees on the lawn. Cars at the curb waiting to pick up students. Voices, car horns. Groups of girls. Groups of guys. A couple smooching against a wall, as tight as if they're glued together.

I never see Laith with anyone. He's a loner, by choice I think—not like me. Always an observer. I'm surprised that he wants to walk me home.

"Hi," I say, anxious to be on my way. Since the TV program last night there might be news about Adam.

"Hi," he says back.

We start walking quickly, with me leading the way.

"I had an idea, after seeing that program last night," he says. "That Chuck Harris guy said your brother might be with a girl named Sari."

"So?"

"If he is with her, someone would have reported her

61

missing, too, right? Unless . . . unless she's using a false name."

"Why would she do that?"

He doesn't look at me. "If she wanted to hurt your brother she certainly wouldn't go by her real name, right?"

I stop in the middle of the street and stare at him. "Right!" I get a terrible ache in my throat. If the girl Adam's with isn't named Sari, that makes it even harder to find him. "But why would she want to hurt him?"

"Envy? Jealousy? Hatred . . . I don't know."

An alarm goes off in my head. "Hatred?"

"We live in dangerous times," Laith shrugs.

Now I feel uneasy. Even though he's no longer in Israel, Laith is a Palestinian, an Arab. The enemy. Why is he trying to be a friend? Does he know more than he's saying? Why should I trust him?

"When I lived in Palestine I never had any Jewish friends," Laith says, changing the subject.

"In *Israel*," I correct, on my guard now, "I never had *Arab* friends, either."

"Here, we could be friends."

"You think so?"

"Don't you find it hard living here?" Laith kicks a stone

on the street, following it and kicking it again. He doesn't look at me.

"You mean—not having your family or friends here? Being made fun of for your accent? That sort of thing?"

A school bus lurches by leaving a thick smell of gas fumes. I stiffen and for an instant realize that since Adam's disappearance I check out who's on the street wherever I walk, what cars slow as they pass, who's on the bus I take.

Laith shakes his head at my question. "Everything here is different from home. That's what I mean. There's so much choice! You go into stores and it's hard to choose; there's so much to see! There's so much freedom. Boys and girls get along so easily with each other. There are so many different kinds of people here, and somehow they mostly get along." Laith's eyes glitter, as if he's seeing a kind of magic. "Everything seems so reachable and ready for one to grasp!"

My whole heart and mind are filled with worry about my brother, and Laith is talking about fitting in. Who cares! He should be sharing these thoughts with a close friend, not me. We cross the street and enter the residential area where I live. The Spanish style house we're renting lies ahead, and I want to hurry inside for news of Adam.

Laith does not pick up on my irritation. "My religion and education teach me to distrust such openness," he says. "My parents see it as—corrupt."

"Corrupt?"

"I'm afraid to go home again. I've changed. And they will not have changed. I won't fit in."

I can't concentrate on what he's saying because Ima is watching from the living room window. "This is where I live, Laith."

He seems to be coming out of a dream when he looks at our house with its yellowing lawn. He seems vulnerable, and for an instant I realize how much he has revealed of himself and how cold I must seem cutting him off. "I'm sorry, but I have to go in now," I say. "There may be news of my brother."

"Oh." He sounds disappointed.

"Thanks for walking me home. I'd ask you in, but right now . . . you understand." What I say is so inadequate, but Ima is waiting. "Maybe we can talk again, at school." I hurry down the path to the front door, eager to get inside.

When I glance back Laith is watching. He calls something to me but I don't hear it, and then he turns and walks away.

Chapter 8

"You're home!" Ima cries, as I open the door. Her face is flushed, her eyes bright. She hugs me, almost dances me across the floor.

"What? Is Adam back?" My heart thumps with excitement. "They've found him?"

"Not quite." She smiles and takes my hand. "Perez phoned. Harris' interview has brought results! They're getting dozens of calls from San Diego, Oakland, Pasadena, Malibu, Huntington Beach!"

I drop my books and sit down. "He's been seen in all those places?"

"No, no! Of course not!"

"Then what?"

Some of the color drains from Ima's face. "It means people are trying to help. Most of those sightings are probably wrong. You know—someone notices a teen-aged boy with dark curly hair walking with a girl and thinks 'maybe!' But—even if only one is true!"

Her voice fades. She needs this tiny shred of hope to go on, and my doubt has dimmed that hope. "You don't believe it," she says.

"It's just that . . . Mom! Are the police going to stop every teenage couple walking together on the street and ask for I.D.?"

Ima runs a nervous hand through her hair. "All right. So, maybe that will come to nothing. But the police are following up on every lead. They even . . ." She stops and frowns. "Even are checking out a report of a boy, who seemed drunk or on drugs, being helped into a house by a man and woman."

I shiver. Could that be Adam? Drugged? Maybe beaten? No, no, no! It's probably their own son.

"Has anyone reported their *daughter* missing?" I ask. Ima looks puzzled. "If Adam *is* with a girl, as the waitress said, she might be reported missing, don't you think?"

Ima thinks for a second, then nods.

I have to *do* something. Something that will help, instead of standing around just talking! "I'm going to check the computer again. Maybe there's something new." I get up and head for Adam's room.

Ima follows me. "Who was that boy I saw you with?"

she asks.

"A kid from school."

"He looks like—an Arab."

I glance back. "He is."

"Oh, motik! Aren't we having enough trouble without you hanging out with Arabs?"

"Arab, *singular*, Mom. And don't worry. We're not 'hanging out.' He just walked me home. No big deal." I sit in front of Adam's computer, type 'Samson' to get on the Internet, and click into his e-mail. Ima draws up a chair to sit beside me.

"It is a big deal, Netta," she says. "Adam's disappearance could be due to some hate group. Skinheads, maybe. An Islamic group."

I get a chill down my neck and swing around to glare at Ima. "An Islamic group? Here, in America? I thought you and Abba said that's not possible."

"Not *likely*. But Perez doesn't rule it out, especially because of your father's job. The satellite work he's doing could lead to better detection of weapon storage in Arab countries. Taking Adam could be retaliation. Could be their way of warning. Of trying to stop the work . . ."

Ima leans toward me, tense and anxious, seeking

reassurance. But I can't give it to her. "Then why aren't they announcing it?" I ask, swinging around to look at her. "You know how the Intifada works! When they bomb something or kill someone, they want the whole world to know what they did and why. That's how it is back home. No! I don't think that's it. Adam was seen in that coffee shop with a girl and they left the shop together. I think he's fallen in love. He knows Abba and you would make him come home if you knew."

Ima sinks back in her chair, drained, as if all the air has been drawn from her body. "Maybe the girl is the bait that trapped him," she says after a while, her voice low and hopeless.

I cover my face with my hands and shiver. Could that be true?

. . .

All during the next hour I read Adam's incoming e-mails but a part of my mind can't put aside what Ima said. If Sari—or whatever her name is—is part of an Islamic terrorist group . . . ? If they assigned her to get to know Adam at school or on the Internet . . . ? If they ordered her to pretend to fall in love with him and make him love her . . . ? If they met somewhere and he was ambushed by her friends . . . ? But then—why haven't they contacted Ima and Abba with their demands? None of it makes sense.

I open an e-mail from Elly-gant. "I haven't met Adam," she writes in answer to my question a few days ago. "Why do you ask?"

"I wrote you three letters and you haven't answered. Don't you like me?" writes Eve.

"I'm beginning to think life would be easier in the army," Adam's best friend from Israel writes. "Yesterday, my neighbor's six-year-old boy, just standing on the balcony looking at what was going on below, was shot! I'd feel safer in the army with a rifle in my hand!"

"I hate to tell you bad news, Adam," another friend writes, "but that bombing in Tel Aviv—the teen night club hangout? We were there once? Well—it was awful! Remember Natasha Kaplan? Pretty blonde, from Russia? She lost an arm. She was with Yuri Gold. He wasn't so lucky."

"Sixteen, seventeen incidents like that each day—on a 'good' day . . ."

I feel tears starting down my cheeks as I read that last letter aloud. "When will all this hate end?" Ima asks. "We are all sons of Abraham, Jews *and* Palestinians. Why can't we get along?"

Ima leaves to start dinner while I check over the remaining letters. There's another report from an Arab-Israeli dialog group. Adam must have spent time discussing issues with this group. Maybe that's where he met Sari.

There's a Peace Camp in Maine, I read, where each summer a few hundred Israeli and Arab teens fly from their homes in Israel, Egypt, Jordan, and the Palestinian areas to spend three weeks together. "An enemy is one whose story we have not heard," is the camp theme. Friendships grow from airing grievances and discussing differences. When they return to their homes many of those friendships continue by e-mail and even with visits to each other's homes.

Except now, with so much violence, Arabs aren't allowed out of their villages in the West Bank and Gaza to go to work, much less to visit a friend in Israel.

As I read about the camp I remember what Joel said—that Adam belonged to some kind of group like that at school. And he made enemies by arguing too loudly about Israel's rights in the Middle East. It sets me thinking.

Could Joel help me sit in with that group? Could Sari be a member? Could Laith have contact with any Islamic or Arab groups?

Chapter 9

I realize Ima has lost weight as she changes clothes before going to the police station with Abba. Her pants hang loose around her hips. She's stopped using makeup and her eyes are bloodshot. Abba, meanwhile, has gained weight and is smoking again. He always eats more when he's got a hard problem at work.

"Can I go with you?" I ask.

"You have homework," Abba says, stubbing out a cigarette and reaching for a handful of peanuts in a bowl.

"And someone should be here to get the phone," Ima replies. "Ben! Do you have to eat everything in sight?"

As soon as they leave I take out my homework and try to concentrate, but the house is different with Ima and Abba gone. It feels empty and threatening. I imagine black-masked Arab terrorists trying to break in. I'm beginning to suspect that maybe Adam's disappearance has to do with being Israeli, or maybe with Abba's work, which could pinpoint where the Arab terrorists store weapons. If Adam was kidnapped—why not me?

In the quiet I hear all kinds of sounds I never heard before—the kitchen clock ticking; a scratching sound from Adam's room like someone is at the window; a creaking, like footsteps, on the loose floor boards in the hall. My heart pounds and my mouth goes dry. *No one's here*, I keep telling myself, but I don't believe it.

I lay my homework aside and open my violin case. Maybe music will drown out the creepy sounds. I ache with longing for the evenings of music together, all of us—Adam, our audience.

But even as I practice the scales, my ears are tuned elsewhere.

With each minute the doubt grows worse. I could throw up, from fear. I finally lay aside my violin and decide to find out who's in the house, no matter what.

I tiptoe from room to room, holding a pair of scissors like a sword in my hand. I open each door and switch on the lights. My parents' bedroom, the bathroom, the small study, Adam's room. Nothing. No one. No terrorists wanting to capture me as well as Adam. Relieved, I return to the living room, pull the drapes, and put Beethoven's Fifth on the CD player. And then I sit near the phone, hands tightly clasped, waiting for Ima's and Abba's return.

. . .

Two days later there is still no hopeful lead to Adam's disappearance. I hear my parents whisper that the police are flying helicopters over parks and rooftops, searching the Los Angeles river channels—looking for signs of a corpse. A corpse! No wonder they don't want me to hear! The word sends shivers through me and I jam my fist against my mouth so they won't hear me cry. Adam, a corpse? Not my dear, bright, thoughtful, full-of-life brother! I will not believe it! Please, God, no!

That day I arrange to meet Joel, cutting my last class and taking the bus to the high school. He's taking me to the Arab-Israeli discussion group Adam is—was—part of. I don't tell Ima or Abba because they'd be angry that I cut school, and scared, too. It's dangerous, they'd say, for a fourteen-year-old girl to be playing detective. That's for the police and private detective to do. But no one can stop me from trying to find my brother.

. . .

I'm more than a little uneasy as Joel leads the way to a classroom on the third floor, uneasy because I'm not sure what I'll say, or how I'll feel standing in front of these older kids and begging for help.

The school is almost empty now that the last period is over. I try to imagine Adam climbing these same stairs, scoping out the girls, maybe thinking about getting home to check his e-mail. From—Sari? What went on in his mind that none of us knew about?

"I told the discussion leader you wanted to sit in and ask a few questions about Adam," Joel says. "Nervous?"

I take a deep breath. "Very."

"Don't be. They're all good people. The police have already been here so they know what you're likely to ask."

"How come they're mostly kids from the Middle East?"

"The way things are going over there, with all that violence—a lot of families are leaving and moving here to live. These dialog groups are meant to bring the sides together. You know—'an enemy is one whose story we haven't heard.'"

I think of Laith. Airing our differences hasn't brought us together.

I stand for an instant outside the classroom, fighting off the urge to turn and run. Who am I, a junior high kid, talking to these high schoolers? But I don't run. I have to go in there and face them. Maybe someone will know something about Adam that the police weren't able to learn.

It's a biology or chemistry classroom, I think, because the walls are plastered with formulas and pictures of famous scientists. Ten or so girls and boys are standing around, talking. They know why I'm here because Joel set it up with the club leader. A lot of them look like the Palestinian Arabs we have in Israel—olive skinned with black hair—but they could be Israelis, because lots of Israelis look that way, too. After all, we all came from the same tribes, thousands of years ago.

The discussion leader comes towards us, a smile on his face. "Hi, Joel. And—you must be Netta. I'm Bob Robertson. We've been expecting you." He turns to the others and calls out, "Listen up, everyone! This is Adam's sister, Netta. She has some questions to ask us, so let's get started."

Bob asks the students to introduce themselves and tell from what countries they came: Egypt, Jordan, Syria, Israel, and the Palestinian areas of Israel.

Standing before them, I clasp my damp hands to stop them from shaking. I can't remember all the names, but I do memorize the girls' names, wondering if one of them is Sari. Dina is a tall, blue-eyed blonde girl from Egypt, a Christian, she says, in a Muslim country. Adam likes blonde girls. Could Dina be Sari?

Maryam is a small, pretty Palestinian with shoulder length dark hair, and Sonia is an Israeli from Haifa.

"Okay, Netta," Bob says after the introductions. "You've got the floor. Ask whatever you'd like."

"Thanks for letting me come," I begin, feeling the heat rise to my face. I clear my throat and my legs feel like they might give way. "You all know my brother Adam's been missing almost two weeks now. We're going crazy at home, worrying. It's just not like him to go off without saying where he's going!"

Each face is fixed on me. They're listening and caring.

"You've met Adam so you know what he's like. Not a mean bone in his body. He's smart and kind and—funny!" I smile. "Once he came to breakfast with shaving cream hanging from his chin, like a beard! And he teases my mother all the time!" I swipe at tears beginning to blur my vision.

"Some people think he ran away, but Adam never ran from anything. He's just not like that, and he had no reason to go off without telling us!" I swallow a lump in my throat and rush on. "Even if he met some girl, which is what the police think, and he's madly in love and just gone off with her, he'd have let us know so we wouldn't worry! My parents would have understood. Sure, they'd have tried to stop him because he's only been here for three months. He's only seventeen! How could it be love?

"So, what could have happened to him? We need to know!"

An Israeli boy raises his hand. "The last time I saw him was the day before he disappeared," he says. "We were in physics together. He seemed preoccupied."

I lean forward, eager to hear what he says. "About what?" I ask. "Did he say?"

"No. But it could've been about a girl. Someone named—Sara or Sari, or something like that. He didn't say, but I noticed he'd written the name on the back of his hand. When I glanced there, he covered it up."

A couple of the kids grin, but Maryam, the Palestinian girl, lowers her eyes. A surge of adrenalin rushes through me. Does she know something?

"Do any of you know someone called Sari?" I ask, staring at Maryam.

Kids shrug or shake their heads.

"Any of you see Adam since last week?"

"I saw him in the coffee shop near school about two weeks ago, I think. With a girl," Dina says. "I was leaving just as they were coming in."

Joel, seated in the front row, holds up a thumb and smiles encouragement. I lean forward. "A girl? What did she look like?"

"Dark, straight hair to the shoulders, sort of like the way Maryam wears hers. Brown eyes, pretty. Nice figure. Wore jeans and a pink T-shirt. I don't think Adam saw me. Don't think he saw anyone—except the girl."

My pulse quickens at this hopeful news. "Did he carry a suitcase? Did you notice a car they might have gotten out of?"

"No suitcase. I didn't see a car if they got out of one," Dina says. "He had an arm around her like she was his girlfriend. She looked older than him, so I thought maybe it was his sister, or a cousin, not a girlfriend."

But nobody contacted the police to report a girl named Sari missing, I thought.

"Maryam?" I dared to ask. "Can you add anything?"

I can imagine boys find Maryam attractive. She's trim,

with skin like satin and big, dark eyes that seem to hide what she feels and thinks. *I don't like her.* Because she's Palestinian? No. Because she seems cold-blooded. She fixes me with an icy smile and runs a hand through her hair. "Sure. I can add something," she says. "You make your brother sound like a saint. He wasn't."

I'm furious at her use of the past tense. *"Wasn't?* Don't you mean—*isn't?"* I ask.

"Wasn't, isn't. Whatever." She glances around to see what effect her words have had on others. Then she says, "How cute—your brother with the shaving cream beard. But we saw another side. Adam could be self-righteous, arrogant, insulting—a real ass." She nods to the others in the class, expecting their agreement. "Right guys?"

I glance toward Bob, wishing he'll interrupt, but he doesn't so I say, "I guess Adam *can* be loud and insulting when he argues our right to the state of Israel, but that doesn't explain why he disappeared. I'm sorry you don't like my brother. Most people do!"

"Would *you* like someone who's eager to go 'home' so he can go into the Israeli army?"

"What's wrong with that?"

"Israeli soldiers are brutes! Vicious animals! It makes

them feel *big* and *important*, strutting around with their rifles and Uzis so they can shoot poor innocent Arab kids for throwing stones!"

I want to shout, *Those little kids throwing stones are there to protect the Palestinian gunmen just behind them. Gunmen, shooting at Israeli soldiers!* But this is no place to debate the issues that divide us. Instead, trying hard to control the anger in my voice, I say, "It's an honor to serve our country. Even I will go into the army when I'm out of high school!" I take a deep breath. "Look. What has Adam's going into the Israeli army got to do with his disappearance?"

Maryam shrugs. "I don't know, but think of this, Netta. You take our land. You squeeze us into a tiny part of what was once our country. You let Jewish settlers build homes in our villages and send soldiers like Adam to protect them. Put yourself in our place. Would you just sit around and take it?"

I open my mouth to answer but a babble of angry Israelis shout out the things I would say—that we're legally a country, even though Arabs don't accept it, that Jews have been on the land for over five thousand years even though the Arabs have tried to take it during three wars, that the holocaust justifies our need of a state. It's bedlam with everyone yelling at once until Bob throws up his hands and shouts, "Enough! Netta's not here to talk politics. She needs to know if we can help find her brother!"

The room quiets down at last, and Maryam looks pleased at the stir she's caused. She glances at one of the Palestinian boys and smiles.

Is she just having fun pushing my buttons? Or does she know something? Are Palestinian terrorists right here in Los Angeles? Why not? There are all kinds of terrorists in the United States. Terrorists blew up an American Embassy in Africa. They blew up those buildings in New York! They kill people all over the world who fight against their beliefs!

I stare at a picture on the back wall without really seeing it. Is my imagination going wild? Could there be a Palestinian terrorist group in Los Angeles? Could Maryam be involved in it? Maybe even—Laith? Could my brother be their victim?

Chapter 10

"Where have you *been*? I've been frantic!" Ima cries as soon as I open the door. She grabs my arm and pulls me inside. Her face is flushed and her eyes widen with fury.

"What . . . what do you mean?" I mumble. She must have found out I cut school! I feel a guilty grin start at my lips. I've never been good at hiding thoughts I shouldn't have or behavior that my parents would be better off not knowing.

"What do I *mean*?" Her voice rises to a hysterical pitch. "The school phoned! They said you were missing from classes this afternoon!"

"Missing? I just went . . ."

"I don't care *where* you went! You were supposed to be in school!" She grabs me and crushes me to her. "With Adam gone, you must know . . ." She bursts into tears.

"Oh, Mommy. I'm sorry. I'm so sorry. I didn't realize . . ."

She seems so vulnerable, so fragile, and I feel so guilty

at having caused her such worry. "Come, sit with me," I plead. "Please don't be angry. I cut school for a good reason. Come, sit down. I'll tell you where I've been and what I learned."

■ ■ ■

"All right," she says, after I've told her everything. "You've done what I'd probably have done at your age, too. But that's it! Now you tell Officer Perez what you learned and let him take it from there. No more playing detective!" She glares at me, stares into my eyes. "Do you understand?"

"But . . ."

"No *buts*! I want to hear the words! *Promise* you'll not take any more chances, that you'll leave those risks to the police!"

I nod, but she's not satisfied. She wants to hear it. "All right. I promise." But I glance aside because I don't think I can keep that promise, no matter how much I'm forced to agree.

■ ■ ■

Every evening after dinner we watch the news on television. In Israel, even teens keep up on world news, probably because we're a small country and we always have to be on the lookout for things that can harm us.

When Adam was home, I felt secure in being part of my tight family, no matter what the bad news was. But now I can't bear it. Ima and Abba sit apart, instead of on the couch beside each other. We're each in our own shells, unconnected.

There's more fighting in Israel. Another peace conference is ending without hope. Africans are dying from drought and AIDS. South American leaders are stealing money that should go to the people. When Adam was here we had a constant flow of comments about what was going on in the world. Tonight, we are silent.

I get up before the program ends. "I've got homework. See you later."

I go to my room and sit in front of my computer. Stare at it, not knowing what I want to do. Finally, I log onto the Internet and type in "Palestinian chat rooms."

There are lots of articles to read, but I already know a lot about the terrorists from Israeli newspapers. What I want is to talk with kids in chat rooms, like Adam did. Palestinian kids.

How do I do that?

First, I have to create a new e-mail name, a boy's name.

What?

Mohammed.

I smile and get a tingly feeling in my fingertips. That's a good Muslim name.

Now, who are you, Mohammed? Can a nice Israeli girl sound like a teenage Palestinian boy? What will I talk about? *What am I trying to find out?*

I think about that for a moment, then shrug and decide I'll just play it by ear. See what happens. It's probably the way Adam met the girl who may be named Sari.

Okay . . . here goes!

I take a deep breath and click into one of the Palestinian chat rooms. About a dozen people are present. As I scroll down and read what they're talking about, I find it's pretty much like other chat rooms I've visited. What musical groups do you like? What do you think of this soccer player or that baseball player, of this or that movie?

"Hi. I'm Mohammed," I type. "New to Los Angeles, from . . ." I pause. Where am I supposed to be from? "Ramallah, Palestine," I type. "Anyone from L.A. want to talk?" It doesn't occur to me until I send the message that I'm using Laith's hometown as mine.

It takes a few moments after it appears on the screen

before I begin to see answers. Five kids are from the Los Angeles area, two from Ramallah. They ask how old I am, where I go to school, how long I've been in the U.S., if I know so and so from Ramallah, what I think of the latest Israeli atrocities.

I write back that I'm sixteen, going to Central High, that I've been in the country only a month and don't know the persons from Ramallah. I say hateful things about the most recent Israeli mortar fire on a police station in Gaza.

It's as if I've become Mohammed. My hands sweat and my heart beats scared as Mohammed takes over, answering as he would. Or, as I think he would.

But after a while most of the writers sign off or lose interest and there's only one person left.

Ibrahim.

He lives in the Granada Hills area of L.A., which is far enough away from Central High that he's not likely to know any kids there. I hope. He's already read the answers to most of the general questions others have asked, so he doesn't have to go over that ground again. Mohammed is into soccer, Adam's sport. Wrestling is Ibrahim's sport, so I imagine him to be sturdy, muscular, or maybe slender, wanting to be muscular.

We chat about school and how American kids show no interest in the Middle East. We move into our own chat room so others don't read what we say and now it gets more personal. "There's this girl at school," he says after we've been chatting for a half hour. "I really like her."

His confession gives me goose bumps. If he knew I was female and an Israeli he'd never confide something like that.

"American? Or Muslim?" I ask. There would be a difference. Ibrahim obeys the very strict laws of his religion, Islam. No holding a girl's hand, and of course— no kissing. No being alone together in a room. Practically no contact until you're married.

"American," he says after a long pause. "You have any experience with girls?"

"Not much," I answer. "Does the girl like you?"

"I think so. But, what do I do? Ask her out? How do I treat her if she accepts? Can I hold her hand? Would that be wrong?"

"Depends on how important our religion is to you."

"Is it important to you?"

"Yes!" I answer. Except—I mean—being Jewish is important.

"Oh," he says. "I guess you've answered my question."

I'm afraid he's about to end our dialog and I haven't found out what I want to know, so I quickly write, "Did you read about that guy at Central who's been missing over a week?"

"The Israeli? Adam something?"

"Yeah."

"I hear he pissed off a lot of Palestinian kids in some dialog group he belonged to."

I feel suddenly breathless. "You know kids at Central?"

"A few."

"I'm at Central. Maybe I know them."

"They're in that dialog group the missing guy belonged to. You know any of that bunch?"

"Don't know many guys yet. Too new here. About that Israeli kid . . ." I hear footsteps outside my door. I've got to hurry. One of my parents might come in and see what I'm doing.

"Netta?" It's Ima's voice.

"Be right there, Mom!" I call back as I type the final words, "What do you think happened to him?"

"He's roasting in hell," Ibrahim writes back, "I hope they all do—every last one of those Israeli scum."

• • •

"Oh!" I exclaim, aloud. It's as though his words have set fire to my stomach. I want to throw his hate back at him, and it takes all my willpower to keep my fingers from flying over the keys with a reply. But if I hope to keep this communication open I have to write as Mohammed, not as Netta, so I type, "I'm with you, Ibrahim."

Ima raps at the door again. "Netta! I need to talk!"

"Be right there!" I call out and hurriedly write, "Got to go, Ibrahim. Lots more to talk about. Tomorrow? Same time? Okay?"

"Okay, Mohammed. Salaam." he returns. And we both sign off.

Chapter 11

"Some girl named Shoshana phoned," Ima says when I come out of my room. "I forgot to tell you before, because I was so upset. Who is she?"

"Don't worry, Mom. She's in my class. I saw her at the synagogue the night we went. Remember? Did she say what she wants?"

"Something about you going to the mall with her tomorrow after school. She left her phone number. Here." Ima hands me a note.

I make a pained face. It's nice of Shoshana to ask, but how can I hang out at the mall, look at clothes, check out CDs, gossip, laugh—when Adam is somewhere, maybe hurt, maybe being tortured?

Maybe dead.

Ima reads my expression and her face softens. "Go, Netta. It will do you good. Brooding day and night won't bring Adam back any faster." She lovingly smooths a strand of hair from my face. "You've been wanting to make friends, and here's a girl reaching out to you."

"I haven't the heart for it, Mom," I say.

"I know. But go anyway, sweetie. Adam would want you to. And I've been too protective, afraid for you, too. I mustn't do that. Just—be careful. Don't accept any rides. Stay away from the curb. Keep your eyes open for who might be following you."

In other words—have a relaxing afternoon, I think, biting my lip.

I phone Shoshana. She's bubbly and chatty but I find myself gritting my teeth at the effort to show interest. Still, I agree to meet her after school to go to the mall.

■　■　■

The shopping mall is a six block walk from school. Along the way Shoshana talks about everything except Adam, which is good. She jokes about the way our social studies teacher dresses and is sure she's got a crush on Mr. Morris, the assistant principal. She tells me her music teacher is having a student performance at his home next month and would I like to come? She's been studying flute for four years. Do I play an instrument?

"Violin," I say. "My parents and I used to play together each Friday night. Ima at the piano; Abba at the cello.

Adam . . ." I can't finish the sentence. Just saying his name brings a lump to my throat.

"What?" she asks.

"Adam was our audience," I finish.

"And he will be, again, I bet! When he's back," she adds, cheerily. "I can't believe anything bad has happened to him."

"I hope you're right."

"If your parents wouldn't mind, maybe I could play with you sometime. Wouldn't that be a blast? A quartet!"

We buy Häagen Daz ice cream at the mall, coffee and chocolate for me, pistachio and vanilla for Shoshana, and stroll along, licking our cones and making small talk. Clusters of high school kids are there, just hanging out, as well as young mothers with strollers and small children. My mouth waters at the smell of Mrs. Field's wonderful chocolate chip cookies baking nearby.

We stop to gaze in the windows of different shops and Ima's warnings and my own fears make me check the reflections in the glass of whoever is behind me. When we pass an entrance to the mall from the parking lot, I scan who's coming in.

It takes a while before I begin to feel safe and relax.

"Oh, look!" Shoshana exclaims as we pass a boutique. "Don't you love it?" She points to a mannequin in the store window who's wearing a short, low-cut black dress and four-inch stiletto heels.

"Cool!" I exclaim. "My Mom would have a fit if I brought that home."

She giggles. "Let's go in and try it on!"

We each take a dress—hers black, mine red, and head for the dressing room. We shed our school clothes and slip into the silky dresses. We examine ourselves in the mirror and inspect each other.

I stare at my Reeboks and grimace. "Needs those four inch heels! And red?"

"But it's great!" Shoshana rolls her eyes. "Red is your color!"

"You think so?" I turn this way and that, trying to decide. Then I glance at her. "Oh, Shoshana! You look gorgeous! Like a model!"

We hug each other and dance up and down, giggling, until the saleslady knocks at our door and asks if she can be of assistance.

"We're fine, thanks," Shoshana calls back, and we stand there, arm in arm, grinning at ourselves in the mirror.

We spend another hour trying out cosmetics. Shoshana complains that her hair is frizzy and asks what shampoo I use. I want to know what color lipstick she wears. We sit for free make-overs at the Estée Lauder counter and when we leave we almost strut, we feel so grown up and pretty.

"This has been fun," I tell Shoshana. "I mean it! For the first time in a long time I haven't been thinking of Adam. Thanks."

And that's when, like a bad omen, like God is reminding me that I have no right to forget my brother even for a few hours, I see Maryam coming towards us, one of the guys from the dialog group at her side. Our eyes meet.

For a moment I freeze, my heart pounding. Has she been following us?

"Let's go!" I say, swinging around, pushing rudely by shoppers to hurry in the opposite direction.

"Netta! Wait! Where are you going?" Shoshana calls, running after me.

I duck into a nearby shop, out of breath, peering around the corner. When Shoshana catches up she says, "What's going on?"

I'm shivering. "There's a Palestinian girl from Adam's

school who may be following me. I spoke with her yesterday and she despises my brother."

"So?" Shoshana stares at me. "Why are you running from her? We're at the mall. What harm can she do?"

Of course, she's right. But reason has nothing to do with fear. "I know it's crazy, but I just couldn't help it," I tell her. "As soon as I saw her, my whole body screamed 'Run!'"

"Oh, Netta!" Shoshana touches my arm, sympathetically.

"I've got to get home," I say. "I'm sorry. It's hard to understand, I know, but every day there's no news about Adam is like a nail being hammered into his coffin. I ache all the time, wanting to *do* something! My parents are worried and afraid all the time. Afraid for Adam. Afraid for me. If it happened to him, it could happen to me because it's not normal for someone to disappear, just like that!" I snap my fingers. "Where is he? Is he alive?" I feel tears slide down my cheek and angrily wipe them away.

"Sssh . . . It'll be okay," Shoshana says. She looks uneasy, like she doesn't know what to say that would help.

Yeah, right. It'll be okay. Everyone says that.

"Look, I'm sorry if I scared you. I'll ask my parents about the recital," I say, calmer now. "Maybe, when life's normal again, we can include a flutist in our group. That would be fun." I try to smile. "Thanks, Shoshana, for calling me."

I start home, walking fast, uneasy about having been out of touch with my family all the hours of school and these few hours more at the mall. I can't wait to get home. There has to be news about Adam! There just has to be!

Chapter 12

It's almost a month now, and each day there's less to hold on to. Our private detective is checking out Palestinian groups, but so far it's led to nothing. Reports from people who think they saw Adam have slowed. Perez says the police are following every lead, but the trail is growing cold. He also says no one has reported a missing girl of Sari's description. Abba believes they're losing interest, even though he goes to the station every day, cajoling, demanding, begging that they keep at it. The problem is, they have too many new cases each day and not enough staff.

In desperation, I went into Adam's room yesterday. There were no new e-mail messages because he hasn't sent or received mail since he disappeared. I roamed around the room, picking up this and that—his hairbrush, for instance, and feeling, through my fingertips, the grasp of my brother's hand on it.

I opened his closet and stared at the clothes hanging

there—two sports jackets, khaki trousers, jeans, T-shirts, his soccer uniform, two tennis rackets, camping gear, and a backpack. I slid a hand into each pocket hoping to find something—and knowing there was nothing because we had each checked Adam's closet before. Finally, I gathered his jacket to my face and closed my eyes and smelled Adam. Smelled that aftershave lotion. Smelled something sweet and strong that was my brother. And I sat on the floor in the closet, among shoes and hiking boots, and cried.

■   ■   ■

Friday night Ima says we are going to services at the temple. "The three of us!" She raises her hand to stop Abba from objecting. "Don't argue, Ben, just go get dressed. We're going, whether you believe in prayer, or not!"

Abba is a scientist. His idea of creation comes from Darwin's theory of evolution, not from the Bible. Religious rituals bore him. At home, he only went to services on important Jewish holidays like Yom Kippur or Passover, always under pressure. He says it doesn't make him any less a Jew. If Israel were attacked, he'd be one of the first to defend it.

Right after dinner we drive to the synagogue, as silent as strangers. I don't know what I hope for. A return to the way we once were, I guess. I miss Abba's lopsided grin when he sees me dressed up. I hunger for Ima's arms around me, for the sound of her humming tunes she makes up. Where is the connection we once had to each other?

■ ■ ■

We don't linger outside where so many families gather before the service, exchanging news and small talk. We go directly into the sanctuary and take seats in back.

"Did you see the flyer on the wall?" Ima whispers to Abba before the service begins. She's referring to the poster she brought in weeks ago, with Adam's picture on it and phone numbers to call.

"Much good it does," Abba says.

Ima's lips set in a hard line. She pulls a prayer book from the back pocket of the seat in front of her and pretends to read it.

I try to concentrate on reading the Hebrew text but keep picturing Adam at my Bat Mitzvah as I recited my part of the Torah. His eyes were so full of love and pride that at one point, when I looked up, I nearly lost my concentration.

After the service, as is tradition, people turn to each other and say, "Shabbat Shalom!" extending a hand in friendship. It brings a lump to my throat because I feel welcome and part of a big family. But Abba whispers, "Let's go." Ima ignores him and follows the crowd from the sanctuary to a room where a table is set with a beautiful flower centerpiece, small paper cups of sweet wine, and a huge challah. We sit in a corner with our drink and bread and although people smile at us in passing, they have their own friends.

"All right," Abba says after a short time, "we came. Now let's go home."

"Ben, sit down," Ima says. "I'm not ready to leave."

I scan the crowd for Shoshana or anyone else from school I might recognize. I'm beginning to feel as Abba— that I want to leave—when I hear my name, and Shoshana pushes through the crowd, pulling her parents along with her.

"Shalom, Mr. and Mrs. Hofman," she says, smiling. I'm Shoshana O'Hara, Netta's friend from school? I'd like you to meet my parents."

Mr. O'Hara is plump and rosy cheeked, almost boyish. He doesn't usually go to temple with Shoshana and her mother because he's Irish Catholic. So maybe he's here tonight to please his wife and daughter.

"We're so sorry for your trouble," Shoshana's mother says. "Is there any way we can help?" She's taller than her husband and wears a dark suit and white turtleneck. Shoshana says she's an attorney.

"Thank you," Abba says. He glances at his watch and stands up. "That's very kind of you, but we're doing everything that can be done."

"I'm an insurance agent," Mr. O'Hara says, ignoring Abba's coldness. "There's been some talk, I understand, that your son might have been taken by Palestinian terrorists."

Abba glances at Mr. O'Hara with sudden interest.

"I have a number of clients from the Middle East. Arabs, Palestinians, as well as Jews. I meet businessmen from the Middle East as a member of the Rotary Club. What I'm leading to is this: Some of these men are more than just clients. They're friends. And we talk about many issues other than insurance."

"So?" Abba prods.

"They trust me. Because I'm not Jewish, I could ask questions you couldn't. Sound them out in a casual way.

Get a sense of whether anyone knows anything about your son's disappearance."

Abba glances quickly at Ima, an excited, wide-eyed look. "You would do that?"

"I would. I saw enough terrorism living in Northern Ireland, because of religious hate. I don't say your son's disappearance has anything to do with a Palestinian terrorist group, but it's not impossible. Fanatics will do unspeakable things."

"Well . . ." Abba lets out his breath and smiles. "I'd appreciate that very much!"

"I'll do what I can. If I learn anything, I'll let you know."

For the next half hour the O'Haras and my parents chat about life in America and introduce us to a few of their friends.

As we drive home Abba says, "Nice people. I like John O'Hara. He has a way of drawing people out. Maybe he'll learn what the police can't."

"Glad you came?" Ima asks.

Instead of answering her question, Abba says, "I feel like taking out my cello tonight. What do you say, when we get home, that we get back to that Vivaldi piece we were working on a few weeks ago?"

CHAPTER 13

At school the next day I find myself smiling. The three Hofmans were a trio again last night, playing together as we hadn't in weeks. Abba lugged out his cello and music stand, I tuned up my violin, and Ima took out her sheet music and sat at the piano. For almost three hours we practiced and played like we used to before Adam's disappearance. All the pieces we already knew and new scores like Vivaldi's *Four Seasons*. We were connected again. I could almost see Adam's grin in the mirror as he'd watch the three of us playing so well together.

"You're smiling," Laith says when we meet in the cafeteria for lunch the next week. Shoshana has a different lunch period, so Laith and I automatically save seats for each other.

"Was I?"

He nods. "You should do it more often. You're—pretty when you smile."

I duck my head and feel a blush burn my cheeks. "I was

thinking about last night," I tell him. "My parents and I play different instruments—piano, violin, and cello, and Friday nights we used to . . ." I choke up and clear my throat. "Do you play an instrument?"

"The mouth organ. You know—harmonica? That's all we could afford."

"I'd like to hear you play sometime." I empty my food tray opposite Laith and push the tray aside. "What do your parents do?"

"They're farmers. We have a grove of olive trees that belonged to our family for hundreds of years. It's a simple life: the trees, a vegetable garden, a couple of goats, and some chickens. We get by—if the Israeli army doesn't come in and level everything."

I point a carrot stick at him. "Our army only levels Palestinian homes and orchards where known terrorists are hiding! The Israeli army wouldn't . . ." Can we ever be friends? No matter what I say he won't believe me. He only sees things from his side, so why bother?

"You were saying?" Laith prompts, watching me with an alertness that makes me think he wants a good argument.

I ache to tell him off but hold my tongue. "Do you

think we can talk about *anything* that won't make you mad?" I ask.

"*Everything* makes *you* mad!" he says. His dark eyes blaze with dislike, and he opens a history book as he eats.

I realize he doesn't intend to speak with me again. And that's not good. In a strange way I like him and need him. He's Palestinian. He's living with Palestinians. He might visit people they know. He might hear talk. Without realizing it he might tell me something that will help find Adam or lead to whoever is holding him. Maybe, if I don't come off like the arrogant Israeli he sees us all to be—and often are—maybe Laith can help.

I don't like myself for thinking this way because I never make friends for what I can gain from them. But we need all the help we can get. Not just from Mr. O'Hara, the police, and the private detective, but from everyone!

"Would you like to come home with me after school and play some computer games?" I ask after a long silence. I pass my lunch dessert, an oatmeal cookie covered in plastic, across the table to him. "I'm on a diet. You want?"

"You're inviting me to your home?" He looks surprised and wary.

"Why not? Like you said, we have more in common with each other than with any of the kids here at school. Of course, if you'd rather not . . ."

He closes the history book and stares at me. Finally he says, "Okay. When?"

"Today?"

"I have homework."

Is this just an excuse because his religion forbids being alone with a girl? "We could do homework together, couldn't we? I need help with math, and you're good at it, aren't you?" I dip a saltine into my bowl of soup and watch him. "In case you're worried, my mother will be home, too."

He thinks about it for what seems a long time and finally says, "All right. I'll meet you after school."

. . .

I phone Ima to alert her that I'm bringing Laith home after school. I explain my reason.

"Are you crazy?" she screams. "Now? When it's very possible those Arabs have your brother?"

"We don't know Palestinians are involved, Mom. That's just one theory." A likely theory, I think, but don't admit it.

The last period bell rings and from the hall telephone I watch kids stream out of the classrooms. "He's just a kid, Mom," I insist. "He's not a suicide bomber coming to blow us up!"

"You're so experienced, you can tell? Netta! I don't want a Palestinian Arab in my home!"

"I can't un-invite him now, Mom."

"Yes, you can!"

"I can't. I'm bringing him, so please be nice. He's the only one, except Shoshana, who's shown me the slightest interest. Maybe, if we get to know each other, talk about our differences, we can become friends instead of enemies."

"Netta!"

"I'm bringing him, Mom. Bye!" I hang up.

. . .

It's not easy chatting about school with Laith as we walk to my house, because part of me is worrying about Ima. What if she turns him away? What would I do then?

"I'm home!" I call, as soon as I enter the house.

"Be with you in a minute!" Ima calls back.

Laith's eyes travel over the shelves of books, the paintings on the walls, the Persian rugs my parents got from trips to Turkey. He goes to the books and traces the spines with a finger, turning his head sideways to read the titles and authors. When he turns to me, he smiles.

"Come, I want to show you something," I say, leading the way to the living room where the piano is open and piles of sheet music lay on the bench. Ima must have been practicing.

I show Laith the photos on the fireplace mantel. "These are pictures my father took of Adam and me at my Bat Mitzvah on Masada." I smile at the photo because Adam has an arm around me. "Have you ever been to Masada?"

"No."

"It's where the Jews held out against the Romans in the first century and died, rather than become slaves."

Laith says nothing.

"This should interest you." I hand him Abba's collection of Roman coins, mounted in a big picture frame. "My father found these when he was a boy, on the beach in Ashkelon. Isn't it weird, holding money that someone two thousand years ago held, maybe used to buy a horse?"

Laith nods and studies the coins. "My father found part of a Roman floor on our land. Small black and white stones in a geometric design. He said our family lived in that area even when the Romans were there."

Here we go again, competing for who came first, who has the right to the land. I almost blurt out, "Jews, too," and stop myself.

Laith carefully replaces the framed coins just as Ima comes into the room. I introduce them and tell her that we're going to do homework together and play some computer games.

"Fine," she says, barely glancing at me or Laith. "There's juice and fruit in the kitchen. Excuse me, but I have things to do."

"She doesn't like me, does she?" Laith asks as I turn on my computer. I am careful to leave the door to my room wide open.

"It's not you. She's preoccupied. She spends a lot of time at the computer, hoping she might stumble onto some evidence, some unlikely clue that might help us to find Adam."

"Anything new on your brother?"

"No."

"Let me try something."

I trade chairs so Laith can take over at the computer. In a short time he's entered a Palestinian chat room that

I didn't know existed. Very quickly he's "talking" with others and not using his real name.

"What are you doing?" I whisper.

"Sssh," he answers. "Just watch."

He glances at the Israeli flag I have tacked to the wall above my computer and starts typing. "I go crazy when I see an Israeli flag," he writes. "My grandfather told me the blue above and below the Star of David means the Jews dream of a Jewish state stretching from the Nile River in Egypt to the Euphrates in Iraq."

"The blue on the flag has nothing to do with our borders!" I cry. "That's just not true!"

"Sssh!" Laith warns. "I'm trying to do something. Watch!"

Within moments after Laith's message goes out answers begin appearing. Almost all curse Israel, believing what Laith wrote to be true. What is he trying to do? Why am I letting him use my computer to spread hate?

All of a sudden the chat room gains a new visitor. Someone named Maryam. My hands get clammy. I point to the screen. "Is she the Maryam from Central High?"

"Yes," Laith answers. "She always comes into the room after school."

Now, the real hate starts.

Kids write in that the Holocaust never happened, that six million Jews were never killed during World War II, that the Holocaust is what's happening to the Palestinian people now.

"Stop it!" I order. "What are you trying to do? If this is what you believe, then leave my house!"

Laith shields the keyboard when I try to reach the keys to shut down the computer. "I have to do this so they'll trust me! Don't you understand? I'm trying to find out if anyone knows what happened to your brother!"

I jump back, as if I've stepped on a hive of bees. My head whirrs with confusion. Should I get my mother? Is he really trying to help? Does he really mean it? Can I trust him?

"Watch! I'm getting to the question you want answered," he says, typing up the next message to Maryam: "Think they'll ever find that Israeli guy who disappeared from Central? Did you know him? Think he's dead?"

I clench my fists, glare at the words forming on the computer screen, and try to believe that Laith means well, that I should trust him even if he is a Palestinian.

"I knew Adam Hofman," Maryam answers. "Do I think he's dead? Yeah. He's the enemy. Isn't that what we all want?"

I jam a fist against my mouth to stop from screaming.

"Sure," Laith writes. "A little revenge for what his father's up to here. Kill the kid and maybe Daddy will go home."

My heart is pounding, part from fear, part from horror. *Oh, Laith! I was beginning to really like you, but how can you say these terrible things?*

"So your question is," Maryam writes, "Did Adam Hofman die at the hands of Palestinians?"

"That's the word going around."

"Fine. If he is dead, I'll be proud to say we did it."

What can I say to Laith when he signs off and faces me? Does he expect I'll praise him for his efforts? His eyes are expressionless. Does he feel anything?

"Why did you do it?" I grasp the back of the computer chair with both my hands, so hard that my fingers ache.

"To help you . . . I thought . . ." He stands up and starts toward the door, carefully avoiding me.

I start after him. "Maryam says he's probably dead! How can she say that? Does it mean she knows?"

"She didn't say, but it could be true."

"Killed by your people?"

"Ever think of the dozens of young Palestinians who die each week at the hands of Israelis?"

"Get out of here!" I say, lunging at him and pushing him into the hall. "Go away. I don't ever want to talk to you again!"

CHAPTER 14

When Laith leaves, I run to the study where Ima is on her computer and explain what happened. "I believe he was trying to help us, but the things he said! So full of hate!"

"I told you I didn't want a Palestinian in our home!" she cries. "You should have known you couldn't get help from an Arab!"

When Abba hears, he closes his eyes and shakes his head. "We don't trust them. They don't trust us. They hate us. We hate them. Where will it end?"

"But what about what Maryam said about Adam?" I ask. "Is he . . . ," I can barely get the word out, ". . . dead?"

"My son is *not* dead!" Ima whispers.

"Abba?"

"I don't know, Netta."

■　■　■

That night Joel phones to ask how I'm doing.

"Fine," I say, automatically. Suddenly my throat

tightens and I'm short of breath. I mumble, "Can't talk. Sorry," and hang up.

Ten minutes later he calls again and now words just gush out, tumbling all over themselves as I tell about Laith's visit. Joel listens without a word. "Wasn't he awful?" I ask, choking up again. "And the others? I hate them all!"

"Don't be so hard on your Palestinian friend," Joel says. "It's amazing he'd take a chance against his own people to find out about Adam. Sounds like he genuinely meant to help you, even if he did use words you didn't want to hear."

I swallow a lump in my throat, close to new tears. "So what did he find out? That Adam is probably dead!" I start to sob. It's so awful I can't stand it.

"Aw, Netta," Joel says, softly. "I'm sorry."

"What can I do? What can I do?"

Joel doesn't answer.

"He's been missing so long! Tell me! What can I do?"

"I don't know, Netta. Wait and hope, that's all, I guess."

∎ ∎ ∎

When I go to school the next day I avoid Laith. He sits alone at the usual lunch table and I pass, barely glancing

116

his way, to take a seat elsewhere.

I sit at a table with four girls, one from my gym class. She nods, then goes on chatting with her friends about a TV movie she saw. I eat in a hurry, wanting to get away by myself, when one of the girls turns to me and asks, "Have they found your brother yet, Netta?"

"No." I sip my milk, avoiding her eyes.

"Oh," she answers, and goes back to chatting with her friends.

I quickly finish my lunch, pack up, and leave, not making any effort to be friendly. I'm so wrapped up in sadness that I no longer care about fitting in. If only I could be with my real friends, back home. Their e-mails come regularly, and they try to comfort, but it's not the same as hearing their voices and knowing they're crying with me.

We are in limbo, which means, I think, that we're in some middle place, not here, or there. Abba is even talking about going home because he can't concentrate. When I say, "Yes! Please! Let's go!" Ima says, "We can't. Not until we know."

Chapter 15

Laith and I are talking again. I go back to sitting with him at lunchtime because maybe Joel is right. He meant to help.

Neither of us brings up what happened at my house. Instead, we talk about our best friends at home, books we've read, trips with our classes or families.

"Did you ever swim in the Dead Sea?" he asks one day after lunch as we sit under a pine tree on the edge of the football field. He takes his harmonica from his backpack and examines it.

"A long time ago," I answer, tracing the smooth seed pod of a pine cone with a finger. "I must have been five or six, and Adam held my hand and took me in to swim. But you didn't have to know how to swim because the salt held you up!"

"And when you got out of the water you itched all over, right?"

"Right!"

"I was about that age when I swam there, too," he said. "I went with my uncle and cousins. Maybe we were there the same day. Wouldn't that be strange?"

"I had a ball, and I remember playing with a little boy. Maybe it was you."

He smiles, closes his eyes, and brings the harmonica to his lips. He blows a scale a few times, wipes the instrument, then plays. Lovely Arabic melodies. I feel like I am back in Israel, in a souk, an Arab market, where music like this floats out of different shops. I can almost see the narrow street with the ancient trough down its middle, the many open stalls, and the people. I can almost smell the spices, the fresh fruits and vegetables, and see the colorful mix of Arabs and Jews who shopped together peacefully for the everyday items of life—until hate turned to violence and fear kept people away.

As Laith plays, students gather, sitting on the grass nearby to listen, their eyes fixed on his face. A few girls get up and dance, moving sensuously and giggling. I am proud of Laith, glad for the attention he is getting.

We walk back to classes when the bell rings, with two seventh graders following along. "I got a really good harmonica for my birthday," one boy says. "I could bring

119

it to school tomorrow. Maybe we could play together? Show each other some tricks? Want to?"

"Sure," Laith said. "That should be fun."

"You were good," I tell him when we part. Suddenly I feel shy.

He manages an embarrassed grin.

But something has changed in our relationship. I am fearful that he will make other friends and won't need me. It's unreasonable to think this way because he has every right to have more than one friend. It's what we both need. But I don't want to lose him. I need him, as fragile as our friendship is. Those are the thoughts that worry me as I make my way to my next class.

"Netta?" my history teacher asks as I pass her desk.

"Yes?"

"You're wanted in the office."

For an instant I stand still, staring at her as she hands me a permission slip. I find it hard to breathe. Why would I be wanted in the office? It has to be bad news.

I turn around and push my way by incoming students, my mind racing. Something has happened to Ima or Abba! There's news about Adam. *Please, God,* I pray silently, *please let them be okay!*

I don't even see Shoshana as I pass her in the hall. She runs after me, "Netta, are you okay?" she asks.

"They want me in the office," I say, running on. "It must be about Adam!"

"I'll go with you."

The office is the usual busy place with students waiting to see the counselor, a girl at the counter explaining to the clerk why she's late, a parent with a son, a teacher collecting his mail. I wait impatiently for my turn to ask why I'm wanted when Mr. Morris, the assistant principal, comes out of the office. "Netta Hofman?" he asks, glancing around.

I grip my books and go to him, trying to read by his expression what he wants.

"Come with me."

Numb with fear, I follow him, waving goodbye to Shoshana. I'm certain I'm going to have to face something I'm not ready for.

Chapter 16

Ima and Abba rise from their chairs as soon as I enter Mr. Morris' office. The news is written all over their faces. The principal closes the door and leaves us alone together.

My parents hold out their arms and I run into them. *Don't say it, please don't!* I beg silently, taking deep gulps of air and hearing strange strangling sounds coming from me.

"Sssh, sssh," Ima croons, swaying, rocking, clinging heavily to me. We hug each other and cry, and they don't say what I can't bear to hear, and then together we walk out of the office.

Mr. Morris guides us through the line of counselors and aides who stand aside as if they know, because they make a path for us. "I'm deeply sorry," Mr. Morris says, as we leave the building. "I hope they find who did it, soon."

"He's dead, isn't he?" I ask. "Tell me. Where did they find him? Do they know how it happened?"

"Not now. When we get home," Abba says. His voice

is muffled as if each word hurts. We hurry home without speaking a word.

As soon as we get into the house Abba pours himself a drink and swallows it in one gulp. Ima has dark circles under her eyes. She drops onto the couch and presses her hands on her thighs.

"Someone reported seeing a car in one of the canyons off Angeles Crest Highway," Abba explains. He wipes tears away with the back of one hand. "There was a young man and a young woman in it. The girl was at the wheel."

"Are they sure it was Adam?"

"Yes," Ima says, "and your father identified . . ." She gulps and doesn't finish the sentence. "It must have happened the day he disappeared. His wallet was missing with his I.D. and money."

I nod and hug myself, trying to squeeze the pain away, but it's not possible. Tears run down my face and I wipe them with my sleeve.

"And the girl?"

"A Palestinian girl from Jerusalem, Sari Mahout."

So, Adam *was* with a girl. The girl must have been alone in the US; otherwise, someone would have reported her missing. I try to imagine what happened those last moments. Did he distract Sari while she was driving? Was she driving too fast? Where were they going? Was the girl one of those Muslims willing to die for their cause—to rid the world of one more Israeli soldier?

I try to absorb what Abba is saying. Somehow, it doesn't sink in. After all these weeks—this is what it comes to?

"Something we haven't told you," Abba says. "Before the car went over the embankment, Adam was shot."

"Shot?" I feel terribly cold suddenly and almost throw up. "And the girl?"

"Not shot, but dead," Abba says.

"Terrorists?"

"The police are checking. Your friend's father—O'Hara—says the people he's talked to from the Middle East haven't said anything that might connect terrorists to Adam's disappearance. Which isn't to say it's not possible."

I'm tired, terribly tired. All I want is to go to my room, curl up in a ball on my bed, and sleep. I don't want to think about what's left of my brother lying in a morgue somewhere—with a bullet in him.

Abba shakes his head and pours another drink.

"Ben, please . . . ," Ima says.

"Could . . ." I stop, as an idea forms, "Why would the killers keep Adam's wallet? Could they use his I.D.? Give some known terrorist another identification?"

Abba's bleary eyes widen. "That's a good question. I'll discuss it with Perez."

"What happens now?" I whisper.

Abba glances at Ima, as if to see if she can handle what he'll say next. "We bury him," he says, softly.

I shiver. "Here?"

"No. Not here. We'll take Adam—home."

Chapter 17

We have been here only a little over three months and think of ourselves as strangers, with few friends. But, as soon as the news breaks, the telephone starts ringing. Not only news reporters but the rabbi and people we don't even know from the temple call to offer condolences. Abba's colleagues send flowers. My teachers and even students from some of my classes send cards. Neighbors knock at our door to bring food and ask if there's anything they can do. The O'Haras come, and Officer Perez. Joel calls. Laith brings a plant called Yesterday, Today, and Tomorrow.

Despite this outpouring of support we are numb with grief and go about our daily life like robots. Ima begins packing for our trip home and cries over each item in Adam's room. Abba spends hours on the phone arranging how to bring Adam with us, calling Israel each day about funeral arrangements and where we'll stay.

I am home from school, helping Ima, but mostly alone

in my room. I can't let go of the question that fills my head all the time. Why? Why would anyone shoot Adam, take his I.D. and money, and force the car, with a woman at the wheel, over the embankment?

That's what I ask Laith when he stops by after school and we circle the block again and again, talking. "I'm sure it's one of your people," I tell him, not even trying to hide my bitterness and suspicion, or caring about his feelings. "Palestinian terrorists. Maybe some of the kids in that dialog group at the high school, like Maryam. And if you're truly a friend, you'll find out, so I can . . ." I don't finish the sentence because I don't know what I'd do. Kill someone, in retaliation? Like we do in Israel after a Palestinian attack? Like they do to us, to get even? Tit for tat? An eye for an eye? So it can never end?

"Netta, what do you want from me? I've been on the Internet. I've asked around. There's not a clue that it's one of *my* people."

"I don't believe it!"

"Why?" His dark eyes flash. "Why are you so sure?"

"For one, Adam was so outspoken about Palestinian rights, he was hated."

"Just because your brother wasn't liked for his

arrogance and his narrow-mindedness about Palestinian peoples' rights doesn't mean someone would kill him."

"What about the work my father is doing? Researching better ways to detect enemy military installations and weapon storage depots! *Enemy*. That means *Arabs* in our own country. Palestinian Arabs. *Your* people!"

Laith shakes his head impatiently. "What makes Adam so special? Lots of scientists are doing what your father's doing, so why would anyone pick on Adam?"

"What about his I.D.? Why take it if they didn't plan to use it?"

"How?" Laith kicks a stone on the path so it scuttles into the gutter.

"You should know!"

"I don't."

"They could give his I.D. to a suicide bomber so he can get past the check points into a restricted Israeli area."

"I.D.s can be forged, Netta. You don't have to kill to get one," he says with a satisfied look on his face. "You know," he says, moving down the street again, "you're so prejudiced you think we're all terrorists. If Israelis and Palestinians are ever to get along, we'll have to learn to trust each other."

Although his arguments make sense, it's hard to let go of what I've believed so long, no matter what he says. For a while we walk on in silence, then I say, "We leave for Israel tomorrow."

"But you're coming back, right?"

"Maybe. I don't know. Depends."

"On what?"

"On whether we learn who was responsible for Adam's death." My throat chokes up, and I'm afraid I'll cry again.

Laith glances at me and then studies the ground. I have the feeling he would like to comfort me but doesn't know how. "I hope you'll come back," he says. "I'd miss you."

■ ■ ■

I hear Abba on the phone. "Hello, Perez. What? *What information?* Have you found them? Who are they? Tell me, *now!*" I draw close to the phone, wanting to hear what the police officer is saying. I can tell by Abba's reactions that Officer Perez won't back down. He wants Abba to come to the station. He has something to tell him that needs to be said in person.

"It must be they've found the assassins," Abba tells us as soon as he hangs up. "Come. We should all go. We need to see those murderers face to face. Learn what drives them to such hate!" He goes to the locked drawer where he keeps a loaded gun.

Ima is pulling on her jacket when she sees what Abba is up to. "No!" she screams, running to him and grabbing an arm. "No, Ben, please!"

My father lifts the gun and checks the safety, shaking off Ima's grip.

"Abba, don't!" I cry, hurrying to my mother's side.

Abba's face wears a stubborn, hard look, like he's too far away to hear anything except what's in his head, yet he hesitates, then slowly puts the gun back and locks the drawer. "Come." His voice is hoarse as he strides across the room to the door that leads to the garage.

I gaze out the window as we drive to the police station, but my thoughts are not on the houses strung with Christmas lights even though it's barely past Thanksgiving yet, the garbage truck clanking its noisy way along the streets, or the small park with preschoolers hanging from bars. I'm thinking of the fury we all feel and our need to do something, like Abba's readiness to kill the assassins, Ima's deep helplessness. My need to pin blame and to find answers that make sense.

I think we all believe the assassins are Palestinian

terrorists, regardless of Laith's assurances. There seems no other possibility.

Now, at last, we are going to find out. And what will we do when we know?

Chapter 18

Perez is on the phone at his desk, but as soon as he sees us he ends his conversation, gets up, and greets us. He leads us past cubicles where men and women are at computers to a room off a corridor. It's so bare, with no windows or pictures on the walls and only a table and four chairs.

"Drink? Coffee? Tea? Cola?" he asks.

"No. Let's get on with it," Abba says, dropping heavily into a chair. Ima and I sit opposite him, eyes fixed on Perez.

The officer shuts the door and joins us at the table. "We have found the boys responsible for your son's death," he says.

"Boys?" Abba leans forward. His hands are clenched so hard they seem bloodless.

"Three. All under eighteen years of age."

Ah, I think. *I was right.* "From Central High?" I ask. "Was there a girl with them named Maryam?"

"No. No girl, and none of them from Central High."

Ima presses trembling fingers over her throat and shakes her head. "Palestinians," she mumbles. "Of course."

"No, not Palestinians," Perez says.

"No?" Abba asks. "So, tell us, for heaven's sake! Who, then?"

"We were almost as sure as you that it was a terrorist act because of your work, Dr. Hofman, and influenced by your certainty," Perez explains. "That is—until we found the car."

"So?" Abba prods.

"The crime lab went over it very carefully for fingerprints and any other clues that might lead us to the perpetrators. Meanwhile, we put the word out for anyone using your son's identification or for anyone boasting of what was done."

There's a knock on the door and an officer looks in. I hear phones ringing and muffled voices. "Sorry," the officer says, and shuts the door.

Perez picks up where he left off. "Your offer of a reward helped, of course. We got dozens of leads, but most of them false. Last night we followed up on a call that led

133

us to these boys."

"You're sure it's them?"

Perez shakes his head. "Positive. We found Adam's I.D. in one boy's wallet. We found the gun used in the shooting."

For a long moment the three of us just stare at Officer Perez. What he's telling us is hard to grasp; it's so different from what we expected.

"Who are these boys? Why?" Ima asks in a gruff, agonized voice. "What did they have to gain?"

"They're from good families," Perez says. "They didn't need the money. It was a random thing, for the thrill. The way they tell it is they cut school and decided to have some fun. They saw Adam and the girl when they stopped for gas and followed them. The girl drove up to the mountains and pulled off at a lookout, presumably to enjoy the view. The boys drove in and parked next to her. Maybe they didn't plan on the killing, but Adam put up a fight. They had a gun so Adam and the girl didn't have a chance."

"Just like that," Abba says.

Perez nods.

Ima starts crying and I reach over to embrace her

though my chest hurts with its heavy load of tears. I shudder at the picture forming in my head. Maybe Adam and Sari were kissing when the boys pulled up beside them. Maybe the first thing Adam saw was a face at the window asking for help, and then a gun and a demand that he and Sari get out of the car. He would have guessed what they would do to his girl and would have fought with every ounce of energy to protect her, until they shot him. Pushing the car over the embankment with the girl and Adam inside would be easy. They probably thought their bodies would never be found in the bushes.

"I'd like to see those boys," Abba says.

"Why?" Perez asks. "I don't think it's wise."

Abba rises from his chair. "I don't need a reason. I don't care if it's wise. I want to see them!"

■　■　■

The three boys are brought into a room with a two-way glass between them and us. They can't see us but we can see them. I don't really want to look, because I'm suddenly afraid. I expect them to have scarred faces and tattoos and sneers on their faces. Still, I look.

They're ordinary kids, about Adam's age. They don't even wear gang colors. They're sloppily dressed, like most high school boys, and one has shaved off his hair and wears an earring. But, you'd never think of them as killers if you saw them on the street. I get a sick feeling in my stomach when one whispers something and they all smile.

All these weeks I imagined every possible scenario, especially that Palestinian terrorists abducted Adam, but never one of just three boys who go out one day for "some fun" and wind up killing.

Chapter 19

We are drained, totally exhausted when we get home. Ima and Abba go straight to their bedroom and lie down.

I knock at their door and ask to come in.

"Come, motik," Abba says.

I climb over Ima to lie between her and Abba. The three of us hold onto each other and finally fall asleep together.

Later, because it is the night before we leave for Israel to bury Adam, I phone my three friends, Shoshana, Joel, and Laith.

"Come back soon," Shoshana says, "and plant a tree with us in Adam's memory."

"When you return," Joel says, "it will be easier. Maybe you'll want to join the school orchestra. You'd make new friends that way."

I think of Adam listening to Ima at the piano, Abba at the cello, and me at the violin—The Hofman Trio. He has on his face such a look of pleasure that I smile at the memory. Yes, getting back to my violin will ease the pain in my heart.

I think of Abba's warnings when I phone Laith. "Don't trust too quickly," he said. I certainly didn't trust Laith quickly. The only reason we connected was because we were both outsiders in an American school. We came from the same part of the world and spoke the same language, so we needed each other. Sure, we argued, but we talked and listened to each other, too. Maybe that's how trust comes, by really listening to others so you can understand what hurts them and they can understand what hurts you. And then, maybe, you can really care enough to be friends.

"I need to apologize," I tell Laith. "You were right. I was so full of prejudice that I couldn't imagine any other reason for Adam's disappearance than that terrorists took him."

"Apology accepted," he says. "Could I ask a favor?"

"Sure, what?"

"When you get to Israel, not right away, of course . . . I know you'll be busy with the funeral and sitting Shiva for a week with your family . . . but if you can, would you phone my parents?"

"What do you want me to tell them?"

"That you know me. That I'm doing okay. That

we're—friends."

I grin at the phone. "Sure. Give me their number."

"And Netta?" There's something breathless in his tone.
"Yes?"

"Uh, uh . . . nothing."

I think he wants to say something that other boys would find easy to say, but his culture doesn't permit. "It's okay. I know," I say.

"Have a safe trip." His voice is gruff.

"I'll call your parents and even visit them, if I can. And Laith? I'll bring back a vial of soil from Ramallah."

I hear Laith clearing his throat.

"And when we return, I'll invite you to the house to hear The Hofman Trio play a special concert—in honor of Adam."